Dear Hng —

Peace & Blessings,
Mara

# the Eye

*Grayce Awakening*

Mara Kerr

BALBOA PRESS
A DIVISION OF HAY HOUSE

Copyright © 2016 Mara Kerr.

All rights reserved. No part of this book may be used or reproduced by any means, graphic, electronic, or mechanical, including photocopying, recording, taping or by any information storage retrieval system without the written permission of the author except in the case of brief quotations embodied in critical articles and reviews.

Balboa Press books may be ordered through booksellers or by contacting:

Balboa Press
A Division of Hay House
1663 Liberty Drive
Bloomington, IN 47403
www.balboapress.com
1 (877) 407-4847

Because of the dynamic nature of the Internet, any web addresses or links contained in this book may have changed since publication and may no longer be valid. The views expressed in this work are solely those of the author and do not necessarily reflect the views of the publisher, and the publisher hereby disclaims any responsibility for them.

The author of this book does not dispense medical advice or prescribe the use of any technique as a form of treatment for physical, emotional, or medical problems without the advice of a physician, either directly or indirectly. The intent of the author is only to offer information of a general nature to help you in your quest for emotional and spiritual well-being. In the event you use any of the information in this book for yourself, which is your constitutional right, the author and the publisher assume no responsibility for your actions.

Any people depicted in stock imagery provided by Thinkstock are models, and such images are being used for illustrative purposes only.
Certain stock imagery © Thinkstock.

Print information available on the last page.

ISBN: 978-1-5043-5625-1 (sc)
ISBN: 978-1-5043-5627-5 (hc)
ISBN: 978-1-5043-5626-8 (e)

Library of Congress Control Number: 2016906831

Balboa Press rev. date: 07/29/2016

# Contents

1. Grayce ................................................................. 1
2. Mrs. Poe ............................................................... 5
3. Planting Seeds ...................................................... 13
4. Sailing ................................................................. 17
5. The Angel Luca .................................................... 23
6. The Angel Frances ................................................ 31
7. Pink Flamingos .................................................... 37
8. Great Abaco ........................................................ 41
9. The Boy .............................................................. 45
10. Horses of Great Abaco .......................................... 49
11. Cottage Sanctuary ................................................ 55
12. The Calm ............................................................ 61
13. The Eye .............................................................. 65
14. Power of the Sun .................................................. 67
15. Josh's Gift ........................................................... 71
16. Saint Lucia .......................................................... 75
17. Lady Palm ........................................................... 81
18. White Pelicans ..................................................... 89
19. Winston Kingsley ................................................. 95
20. Think Love .......................................................... 99
21. Journey Home ..................................................... 101

*This book is written with honor for my mother who taught me how to sail. Thank you. I love you.*

## *A personal dedication to the memory of Dr. Wayne W. Dyer*

When I remember to write from my highest self, act from my highest self, or think of others first I embody all Dr. Dyer's divine, awe-inspiring books have taught me. That honors him now as I pay respect to his mystical legacy. Dr. Dyer's books have always shown me exactly how to improve my own life. His timeless books will always open the door for any eager sage seeking truth.

The dog I purposely named Ranger in, "The Eye" is a beautiful **Namaste to Dr. Dyer.** In his wonderful book, **"I Can See Clearly Now,"** Dr. Dyer wrote about his experience during the summer of 1960, aboard the largest ship in the world, the USS Ranger. After touring naval bases throughout the western Pacific, the mighty ship and crew then home-ported in Alameda, California.

On board the USS Ranger, Dr. Dyer was a communications specialist! No kidding, I think we already knew that part. Bless his amazing soul. Anyhow, the entire crew of 2000 had unexpectedly been directed to go immediately up on the flight deck and give a mandatory salute, "Hi Ike." The salute was for President Eisenhower, who would soon fly over in a helicopter. Wayne was outraged and decided he would not act like a flock of geese for no sensible reason. I truly love Wayne Dyer. He is simply genius at any age.

Dr. Dyer further explains that he is a skilled professional. He is simply unwilling to be herded into a group to stand in the hot sun. He would not salute a man he was not even in alignment with because of war. He refused to participate in a silly and expensive maneuver designed to make a political statement. He teaches us that he is quickly learning how to be, **"quietly effective,"** at twenty years old.

Retreating many decks below, he simply turns to meditation. He writes how he can sit there in solitude until the madness above subsides. Wayne already is teaching us to back away from false demands of ego and then go quietly within. What an exceptionally brilliant, young mind. In the safety of his quarters and bunk he picks up the novel, "To Kill a Mockingbird," and begins to read it for a third time. Wayne writes about his delight in discovering, **"You don't have to be just like everybody else… there is another way."** Bless you, Dr. Dyer your grace spills over to us all.

Dr. Dyer closes the illuminating chapter with an adorable story about sharing his parental advice to his thirteen-year-old son, Sage. Dr. Dyer writes; "If you follow the herd, you will end up stepping in shit. The shit I refer to is, living with yourself when you ignore what is right and true and instead follow the 'offal' instructions of others who are afraid to leave the herd and want you to be just like everyone else." Brilliant advice from a highly evolved parent, and an enlightened master, who speaks only truth.

Today, I like knowing that I am wholly devoted to follow in Dr. Dyer's sacred footsteps. It is a joy to be walking peaceably into divinely inspired service with my own uniquely creative style of writing. I could never ask for more. I am blessed. In his teaching's, we all learn again and again to respect our sacred selves. That self-loving philosophy is the most useful gift I have ever received in my entire life. Thank you again to my favorite author of all time, Dr. Wayne W. Dyer. A divinely inspiring, modern mystic who truly made a difference.

And, an extra thank you to his entire family. You selflessly shared the lovable master with us all. The Dr. Dyer books we all love to read required a lot of time to write. Time you allowed him for writing. His books are truly a divine gift for all readers and fans worldwide. My sincere love is expressed to you all as his daily physical absence in reality, must produce endless tears. Dr. Dyer's divine voice continues to call us all into acceptance and grace, even as we might sit with our grief. I wish you all infinite peace and limitless love.

Peace and blessings,
Mara Kerr

## With appreciation...

I wrote this poem for my first book, "Oceanus, The Infinite Healing Power of Love." This poem is my brand. My pledge. My devotion to all that exists in the natural world. It was written for our Creator. Please enjoy and feel the peace that is in the message.

### The Blue Planet: One Ocean, One Planet, One Chance

*Out of the cosmos came creation,*
*Out of creation came water,*
*Out of water came life,*
*Out of life came love,*
*Out of love came peace,*
*Out of peace came harmony.*
*Without harmony there is no peace.*
*Without peace there is no love.*
*Without love there is no life.*
*Without life there is no water.*
*Without water there is no creation.*
*Without creation, there is only the cosmos.*
*Water is life, without it there is no life, there is nothing.*
*In nothingness, there is only the infinite.*
*In the finite begins an interpretation, so a dream begins.*

*Mara Kerr, 2008*

## Chapter One

# GRAYCE

Grayce strolled down the long, groaning dock to her boat. She recalled the many times her grandfather, Winston Kingsley walked her hand in hand, down this very same dock. Always partially if not fully, stumbling drunk. The pier now released important memories for Grayce. An opportunity, as if every step told a story. She recalled how tall and assured he seemed. She would adoringly gaze over at him strolling next to her. He kind of lumbered along with a sturdy gait that resembled a tired, old horse. She remembered how small her hand felt inside of his large rough and calloused grip. Grayce also remembered how many times he disappointed her by being the town drunk. Winston had a wicked side. Everyone in Key West knew it. Even still, he would be proud she thought. Walking bravely through her confusing mind chatter, she wished her grandfather was here to see this extraordinary day. Grayce always loved Winston without condition. The immense void he left after his passing away was undeniable. Grayce decided to leave that part to herself for now.

Grayce could see the animated crowd ahead. Nervous butterflies started to quiver inside her stomach. What is their absurd interest in me she wondered? It is good to be scared she reminded herself. Keeping in mind what her father, Angus had told her so many times before. He would say, "Being nervous or anxious simply means you are changing. Just think of it like growing pains. Embrace your challenges Grayce. Whatever you do, wherever you go, never stop dreaming." She deeply longed for her father and wished he could see her now. Grayce recollected his haunting words. They now just rattled around in her head offering nothing but confusion. Angus would be teaching her how to ride a pony and say, "Grayce it is time to soldier up, get tough. It is now or never. Wimps do not take home any blue ribbons or trophies." Usually his words only made her cry. She hated admitting this but knew his roughness did toughen her up. It also gave birth to her unwavering independence.

Walking on, Grayce affirmed internally that she had Ranger. He was her faithful, black Labrador Retriever. Ranger never left her side. Ranger was absolutely with her today in every possible way. He seemed to sense the excitement, too. Ranger was her rock, her ground, her certainty. He was the one who never let her down. The one who fed her with unconditional love, from an infinite source. Ranger could ease her thoughts just with his presence. Grayce felt his bouncy stride, nervously quicken, as they neared the crowd. Grayce quietly sent Ranger love. That energy oozed out of her through the leash to him. She felt his walk slow until he completely relaxed. She loved doing this. Unconditional love, it removes all fear. Every single time. Grayce embodied their love. Their unique circle of connection was paramount in her life.

Approaching her boat, she saw multiple photographers taking random pictures. When they spotted her, they turned their attention directly to her. "Look it's Grayce and Ranger," she heard them say. "Grayce, when do you set sail? Grayce, what does it feel like to attempt an epic sail around the world alone?" They aggressively asked question after question until she and Ranger stopped in front of them. She smiled, shyly. It was her Princess Diana smile that Angus taught her. The fake smile would help her win a lead line pony class at the esteemed Palm Beach Horse Show. It always seemed so insincere and phony. Secretly, she really hated this social part. Tuning out her agitation, she tried to exude confidence. People were definitely not her favorite thing. They usually just bored and mainly annoyed her. She tried anyway.

Standing barefoot in the sun wearing her cut off jean shorts, Grayce looked like anything but a professional sailor. "Hello everyone and thank you for coming out today. If you will be so kind to allow me to speak first, I will address your questions. My name is Grayce Kelly Kingsley. I am seventeen years old. This is my sailboat, the *Silent Partner*. Today, I am embarking on a solo journey to sail around the world. For your convenience, I have prepared maps for you all to take and study, if you like. My sail is going to be tracked on Google Ocean. So that is another really cool way for you all to follow my journey. And, there are helpful instructions on using Google Ocean with my map. I'll be stopping at many historical points, they are highlighted. And, I will share my story on a blog and social media. You will not miss a thing as Ranger and I cruise around the earth."

"Many of you already know me and are familiar with my story. For those of you that don't, I have brought a brief outline of my family history. Yes, my Grandfather was the legendary, Sir Winston Kingsley, of Key West. My father was Angus Winston Kingsley II of Palm Beach. This is Ranger my black Labrador retriever. Yes, he is going along with me today on this epic sail. Obviously, I am the captain and Ranger is my first mate." Grayce laughed to herself, thinking how organized the press now imagined she might be. Nothing could be farther from the truth. Grayce prayed she could set sail before anyone discovered she had no clue what she was really getting into. She was an expert sailor, that part was true. But sailing around the world alone?

*Chapter Two*

# MRS. POE

Grayce was thankful for the unwavering support of her amazing mentor Mrs. Poe. She definitely stood out among the reporters. Everyone from Key West was here to wish Grayce, *Bon Voyage*. Standing there in her diamonds and high heels Mrs. Poe always looked out of place on the boat dock. That is exactly why Grayce loved her so much. Mrs. Poe was the first woman to have any kind of influence on the Key West born, tomboy. In times of struggle Mrs. Poe would say, "Grayce give up the struggle. You are always fighting nothing but yourself. Do not ever forget honesty, sincerity, and a touch of love and affection will open all doors for you. Treat people with kindness and they will always give you what you need. Always forgive everything, including yourself." Grayce usually forgot this precious advice. She always intently listened anyway.

    Mrs. Poe ran the little grocery store down on the farthest edge of town in Key West. The eclectic store was called, *Hasi' Gawa' General Store*. Everyone loved Mrs. Poe from the day she arrived so many years ago. She had gently brought the *aloha* spirit to Key West. Mrs. Poe used to tell Grayce fabulous tales about her childhood days of living on Hawaii. Mrs. Poe was also the lucky recipient of three failed marriages to very wealthy men. That part was perplexing but Grayce decided no to give it much thought. Mrs. Poe told Grayce that girls in America have forgotten how to get the doors opened by anyone because they are so busy busting down doors on their own. This always confused Grayce because her father Angus and her Grandfather Winston, always told Grayce to "go charging head first through the door, ask questions later, and for sure never ever apologize!"

It was a lot of discombobulating information always coming at young Grayce. No wonder she now dressed like a boy. Straight legged Levi jeans and a white men's tank top was her staple outfit, only changing for cut off Levi shorts. She had purple streaks in her long, blond hair. Her hair was always braided in dreadlocks. Grayce absolutely never wore lipstick. Shoes were simply not necessary, unless bad weather at sea required it. Grayce knew absolutely nothing about something called shopping. She believed in give and take amongst friends. Grayce needed her boat, her dog, her bargain and exchange system, and the ocean, period. Or so her seventeen year- old mind thought.

Mrs. Poe approached Grayce with a large picnic basket of home baked goodies. She was smiling and crying at the same time, Grayce adored side of Mrs. Poe. She was always showing her dual emotions and mostly perplexing feelings. Grayce's grandfather Winston had always told her to never show her emotions. She was thankful someone had shown her that it was all right cry. Grayce painfully reflected neither Winston or Angus ever baked anything worth putting into a pretty basket, let alone give away as a gift. Naturally, Grayce took home made handouts where she could and definitely always appreciated it.

Grayce took the pretty basket from Mrs. Poe, and thanked her. They exchanged a long teary-eyed embrace. No words would come to mind, they simply weren't needed. Independence and determination fueled Grayce now. Nothing would stop her now, nothing. Confidently, she and Ranger stepped upon the polished, wooden deck of the *Silent Partner*. They both felt at home on the boat, as they should. They had sailed countless hours together with just each other as company. Long hours cleaning the boat together. Long hours waiting for the wind to blow. Long hours pacing the beach. Long hours waiting for the rain to pass. Long, precious hours wasted sleeping. These two loved to sail, it was who they were together, as one.

Grayce bravely looked somewhat suspiciously out among the savage reporters and said she would field three questions only. She pointed to a tall man in front, "You have a question?" she said. He politely asked Grayce about the dangers of being a female and sailing alone. Grayce responded, "I was born to sail and whether I am a female or not has nothing to do with the success of my journey. My skills as a sailor will see me through, period. And, if you must know, I will sail protected by my angels. That is not up for debate; it is simply a fact, period." Grayce secretly felt a sense of insincerity fill her heart. The truth was she was a little scared she would not be tough enough to sail all the way around the world by herself.

"Is there another question?" she said firmly. Grayce pointed to an odd looking woman in a horribly ugly hat standing near the tall man. "Grayce how did you decide on your predetermined locations to stop?" Grayce giggled inside, silently thinking about where she might or might not take a time out. "My plan is to visit many islands of personal interest to me. I will chat about my experiences on my blog. My first scheduled layover is an isle called Great Abaco in the Bahamas. I am going to see the critically endangered herd of Spanish Barb horses living there. Last question?" Grace sheepishly wondered to herself if she would even follow her own plotted course, due to unexpected tropical weather and unpredictable ocean conditions.

Grayce then quickly pointed to a small, elderly woman with a sweet smile at the side of the crowd. "Grayce will you introduce us to your angels?" Grayce smiled and responded, "Well, they do not need any introduction for if you believe they are already visible to you. An angel is simply an attendant spirit, a winged figure in human form. Always superior in intellect, the angel offers its divinely guided assistance to any willing human, anywhere." With that affirmation she quite purposely ended the questions. Grayce waved and said; "Thank you for your support in coming out today. I know you will all be here upon my return. So for now, let us simply know we will see each other again. Peace and blessings to you all. I wish you well." Grayce did have a relentless faith in her angels. That unproved element was what she secretly hoped would bring her success on this daring and exciting journey.

Grayce went right to work preparing the *Silent Partner* to set sail. Hoisting the mainsail filled her with a great excitement. Her confidence soared as she went through the routine she knew so well. Ranger took his favorite position up on front deck of the boat. Ranger delighting in sailing and was incredibly athletic about riding on the boat. Grayce put the love filled basket from Mrs. Poe down below in the tiny kitchen nook. There was an intriguing black book peeking out of the basket that got her attention. It was simply entitled, "Love." She opened the mysterious book and discovered Kahlil Gibran's words:

> *"Life without love is like a tree without blossoms or fruit.*
> *Sadness is but a wall between two gardens.*
> *Trust in dreams, for in them is hidden the gate to eternity.*
> *Love one another, but make not a bond of it;*
> *Let it rather be a moving sea between the shores of your souls." Kahlil Gibran*

Mrs. Poe was always teaching Grayce something about love so the book did not surprise her. She had certainly no time or need for love in her life but enjoyed the thought of Mrs. Poe thinking she did. She mentally assessed her personal supplies and contemplated if she would have everything she needed. Naturally, Grayce was more worried about Ranger's food than her own. She checked the supply cabinet labeled dog food and quietly made another mental note that he had plenty on board. His food was freeze dried so it was not perishable. She smiled thinking what an easy companion Ranger was onboard.

Grayce was just a tiny thing, barely 110 pounds. Her food rations were quite minimal. She was also a strict vegetarian. Fortunately, no meat or dairy was needed for this trip. She had a nice supply of her favorite protein mixes for shakes and lot's of tofu. She would be able to restock fresh fruit and vegetables along the way. Her biggest supply was water for she knew that was the most precious supply of all. She confirmed her precious I-pad was down there this was one trip that would be blogged about everyday. Grayce had an awesome following of friends on Facebook. They were all really anticipating her epic journey. She felt these people online were like a supportive family, even if invisible in the physical world.

Naturally, Grayce knew her most important followers were her angels. They had already been prepared for this trip. She did not really pray so much as have conversations with them. Grayce simply talked to her favorite angels, believing they sailed with her everywhere. Grayce eyed her surroundings one more time. Spotting her favorite pillow, sunscreen, bohemian umbrella set, yoga mat and satellite phone caused a grin. What else could I possibly need she thought to herself? Good weather and predictable winds. That was most important and she knew it.

As Grayce went back up to the deck to start hoisting her jib sail, she admired her quote on the galley door.

***"Never be afraid. The greatest enemy of humankind is fear. Be confident in the love and wisdom of God." White Eagle***

Grayce had been planning this sail for almost three years. Actually, her grandfather Winston helped her plot the course before he died. Grayce would head off the coast of Florida, bravely determined to make it solo around the world. Her strategy was to travel the equator as closely as possible, only veering off for better wind and to pass by islands. She was excited about the first stop in the Bahamas. Angus had been the one to tell her many stories of an island called Great Abaco. She truly wanted to meet the wild Spanish Barb horses there.

Grayce intended to enjoy the cultures she might discover along the way for she knew this sail was not a race. She had placed no time constraints upon herself purposely. She had nothing to hurry back to Key West for anyway. Grayce had been lucky enough to grow up around horses. Her father, Angus, had been a well known horse trainer in Palm Beach. Angus was tragically killed in an untimely airplane crash. The accident was just off Key West eight years ago. Learning more facts about the mysterious horses on Great Abaco searching the Internet one day, she vowed to help out if she could. It was a silent tribute to her father. That part she absolutely kept to herself.

As Grayce reviewed her checklist to complete before sailing, she decided to pull up the weather one last time. She had already consulted the weather channel several times today and everything looked clear. Recalling how many times she and Ranger had gone out for an afternoon sail, only to have to cut it short due to unexpected bad weather. Grayce resolved to check again one last time. *Silent Partner* was outfitted with the most sophisticated weather equipment possible. Winston had done his best before he died to bring the boat's technology up to date.

Actually, Grayce had also found ways to rally her Key West community around her sails. This time was no different, just a much longer sail. Her large base of good friends had always unconditionally supported her sailing efforts. The community had even helped raise money when she needed to update her weather tracking equipment for this trip. She recalled the time when she was only five years old and her grandfather Winston took her out boating only to run across a small hurricane. The two unlikely sailors were tossed around out in the storm for three agonizing days. Of course, Winston was drinking as usual. They all wondered what would become of young Grayce. What would happen if she ever fell overboard?

After that incident, the whole town tried to take away Winston's rights to young Grayce. It didn't work. Winston had been in Key West long enough to wield some authority, even if no one knew why. Grayce's father Angus was always away, at the posh horse shows in Palm Beach. His absence usually fueled Winston's drinking. Grayce was forced to grow up early. Her love for sailing helped create her self-reliance. After that frightful experience with Winston and the hurricane, Grayce became a real fan of double checking her weather programs. It also taught her a lot about trusting her own instincts. One lonely day after cleaning Winston's house boat in the blistering hot Key West heat, she claimed a silent mantra; **"When faced with stupidity, assault it with a higher thought every single time."**

Ranger was perched up front on the polished mahogany wooden deck. Adorably outfitted in his bright red bandana and his yellow inflatable life vest. One of the reporters tried to hand off a bottle of champagne to Grayce, she laughed and politely said, "no thank you!" If there was one thing Grayce knew about the rules on her boat, she insisted no alcohol was ever allowed on board. Her grandfather Winston had literally drunk himself to death. Grayce knew all to well the wicked demons that alcohol would call into a life. She suggested to the reporter that he give the bottle to Mrs. Poe, he willingly complied. Grayce enjoyed showing people she had boundaries. Three brown pelicans flew overhead in a tight circle. Time slowed down.

Everyone knew Mrs. Poe would find something important to link the champagne to. She suggested symbolically breaking the bottle on the front of the boat to symbolize Grayce embarking on her journey. Grayce declined, "Sorry, but I worked too hard on restoring the *Silent Partner* to break anything on it." Mrs. Poe silently understood. "Grayce I will take the champagne home for safekeeping until another special occasion." The crowd gave Mrs. Poe a hearty applause. Grayce just smiled and then gave everyone a silly, sailor salute. Grayce's departing words were simple. "I love you Mrs. Poe."

## Chapter Three

# PLANTING SEEDS

Grayce went about securing the main sail, the jib and the ropes. Firing up the tiny trolling motor she felt her heart surge. The *Silent Partner* began to move along through the docks, heading out to sea through the marina. As she looked ahead, she saw a familiar sight of a manatee momma and baby. She was happy that she had helped create more awareness surrounding these very special marine mammals. She was a part of a special campaign many years ago in Florida. It was designed to create more compassion for the manatees, and Grayce was the poster girl.

It was really fun for Grayce because she had met many celebrities including Jimmy Buffet. She recalled how Winston had taken her to meet Jimmy Buffet at a concert in Key West. It was December and Grayce had made Mr. Buffet a Christmas ornament. She was beyond elated to have the chance to meet Mr. Buffet. Grayce wanted to give him a small Christmas ornament she had lovingly made in his honor. When she handed him the fragile guitar ornament she was horrified. Grayce watched him accidentally, but clumsily drop the ornament on the hard ground. It shattered in many pieces. Tears swelled in young Grayce's eyes.

Mr. Buffet tried to assure Grayce he would fix the damaged ornament but Grayce knew it was ruined forever. She was able to stay in touch with Jimmy Buffet after this incident, for he always remembered dropping the little Christmas ornament. It was like a seed being planted and now it was blooming. Grayce was actually scheduled to meet Jimmy Buffet in Saint Lucia, Barbados. She was certainly looking forward to that. A little Margarittaville never hurt anyone, all Parrot-heads know that. He would be giving a concert there, and she knew she wouldn't miss that for the world.

Grayce looked back across all the people waving to her and tried to make out the faces she knew. There were many. Most of them were smiling and cheering her on. Others seemed to be frozen, just standing there with tears streaming down their face. She tried to imagine how it would feel many weeks later into her sail, when she had been gone for days on end without any contact with another human being. This was one part of the trip from which she unknowingly grew strength, watching all the faces of fellow human beings saying goodbye. The images of the faces would stay with her over the next year, keeping her company in the long days out alone at sea. She picked up her Nikon camera and snapped a few photos of the crowd. She also took a great photo of her faithful buddy, Ranger. The love she felt for him made her smile and a great peace filled her anxious heart. She turned the trolling motor off and the wind filled her sails.

**Ranger proudly sitting up front with the gentle breeze, simply noticed everything passing by. She cherished the smile on Ranger's face because he absolutely relished in sailing. His ears gently flapping as a gust of wind caught the sweet spot and gave way to air. His trust in Grayce and the Silent Partner was not taught, it just was. Love now sprinkled the salty the air. Their combined joy being carried along by the sweet ocean breezes.**

Grayce went and got her I-pad to record leaving Key West into her blog. She felt lucky for the technology available today. She giggled thinking how much Winston would have hated it all. He would have scolded her for bringing the l-pad and camera saying they were unnecessary, a distraction from nature and too bulky for sailing. She sent loving thoughts up to Winston and thanked God for the chance to be sailing today. She laughed thinking how he would have weighed down his journey with boxes of Rum. Along with outdated, mostly useless, astrology charts. To understand the stars all you have to do is stay sober enough to see them. Men, she thought. Simply clueless and dumb.

Grayce had been unknowingly planting seeds for this garden a long time. She had a good plan and with germination it would produce a bountiful harvest. There was also a much larger and more experienced gardener, invisibly planting seeds for her too. In time, she would reap countless bouquets of beauty and grace from this currently unknown gardener. There were epic dangers in the ocean and unexpected weather in every day. Her faith in herself was strong and self willed determination will get you far. Even the best planned gardens can fail though. Time would eventually tell what kind of garden would bloom for young Grayce, out amidst the great sea of blue.

*Chapter Four*

# SAILING

As *Silent Partner* exited the safety of the marina harbor, Grayce felt a great peace sweep over her. She was sailing now and there was no place on earth she would rather be. The wind blowing in her hair and across her youthful face invigorated her soul. The smell of the sweet salt air cleansed her nasal passages. Her breathing just felt easier. Leaving the vortex of all the clingy people behind now felt liberating. She never tired of watching Ranger ride up on the bow of the boat, always smiling and watching for anything unusual. By helping Grayce search for and locate injured manatees, he knew instinctively about navigating the ocean. Ranger was the best first mate ever.

Grayce loved the roll of the boat as it moved through the ocean swells. To her, the rocking of a boat was home. As a baby, when Grayce could not sleep, Angus would walk her over to Winston's boat house and they would take her sailing. It was the only place she slept soundly, on the boat in the waves. They loved telling her stories about how they would stop the boat and Grayce would immediately start crying again. Sometimes they just sailed all day long. They taught young Grayce to swim while she was still in diapers too. It was an accident the first time when they were anchored off the coast of Key West fishing. Grayce was barely nine months old. They would let Grayce crawl around the deck, usually forgetting to keep a close eye on her.

Winston would always be fishing and drinking. Angus would be drinking and reading about the Palm Beach Show Horse society scene. Neither one saw as she crawled right to the edge of the boat and fell off into the warm ocean water. Angus was fortunately right there and jumped right in, but Winston yelled at him to just let her be. They both watched in disbelief as Grayce bobbed up and began to dog paddle with never a tear or cry. They both knew from that day on the ocean was Grayce's home, and it has been ever since. No fear existed on or in the water, instead it was her place of peace.

As the two men spent countless hours down at the marina on their beloved boats, varied experiences shaped Grayce's character. She grew up on the docks and among the local fisherman. It was not exactly the kind of childhood that would rear a refined young woman. Grayce's mother, Frances, had unexpectedly died thirteen years ago in a dreadful horse showing accident. Angus was not equipped at all for raising a child, so he turned to the only family he had, his drunken and disorderly father Winston. When Angus would head back to Palm Beach for horse shows, he would more often than not leave Grayce alone with Winston. The result was Grayce had many friends down on the docks and in the marina. People who you would not imagine taking protective care of a child, did step up and help out whenever it was needed.

It usually does take a village to raise a child, it is true. Grayce always had a natural sense of belonging to extended family wherever she went. This was a gift Winston and Angus unintentionally gave her by raising her in this marina community or tribal style. Certainly there was some obvious weakness and even danger in their haphazard, co-parenting style. There is also a silver lining in everything. Some of the best parts of life and learning simply arrive by accident. Grayce thought it was normal to drop onto someone's boat for dinner, unannounced and unexpected. Always anticipating being welcome because everyone had always treated Grayce like she was family. This was another blessing that growing up on the docks provided her. Grayce had zero fear of strangers because of these unique experiences growing up in Key West.

Grayce checked the weather one more time and saw clear sailing all the way to the Bahamas. She sipped some water and settled in for a few days of smooth sailing. She began to float back into her mind of the days spent sailing with Winston. He loved to take Grayce sailing and enjoyed telling her many crazy stories of fishing life in Key West. He was truly a unique character everyone knew and loved. He was loud and short of temper. Get old Winston mad and there would be a price to pay. He was sincere, however, and if he was your friend you could always count on him to be there. Winston had a soft side that would always shine brightly as Grayce began to mature into a young girl.

Winston had first taught Grayce how to sail on an old small sailboat called a Sunfish. The little boat was perfectly equipped for a young girl to learn the ways of sailing. Winston even encouraged Grayce to tip the tiny sailboat over teaching her to be unafraid of the ocean. Often Grayce would take Winston's old Labrador, Oreo, sailing with her on the Sunfish. Winston would sit on his houseboat with a tall, cold drink in his hand just giggling. Grayce and Oreo sailing around the marina, high siding and then flipping the tiny sunfish for hours on end. Their combined laughter in the marina was like God's perfume sprinkling joy across Key West. Eventually, the golden sun would slowly disappear from the vast horizon. Darkness was the only thing that would drive Grayce and Oreo out of the water.

Grayce also recalled how Winston had taught her to fish so expertly. As if she was going to spend her whole life fishing at sea! The thought made her gag out loud. By the time Grayce was just five years old she could cook a mean batch of a spicy fish soup called Winston's Fire. He was always leaving the cooking up to Grayce, so she just learned to cook without fear of judgment; it was really quite adorable. Winston would take Grayce shopping for all the ingredients and then turn her loose in the kitchen on his old, very untidy houseboat. There were no rules. And a big mess was actually a badge of honor. This style of teaching did lead to a few disasters in the kitchen, but he always said to Grayce, "Dear girl, through pain comes wisdom." Grayce just kept trying until she would get things right. Winston gave Grayce the confidence to learn through failing. Such a wise lesson to teach, she intuitively thought.

Suddenly, Grayce noticed a large school of bottlenose dolphins off the bow of the boat and she smiled. It is an inspiring sight beyond imagination. Hundreds of dolphins in total harmony bringing joy all around. This is exactly why she loved sailing, the unparalleled joy that seeing marine life brought her. Grayce could loose herself completely in witnessing the majesty of the ocean. Winston had been the one to teach her about dolphins, and they always brought good luck for sailing. She watched them methodically swim together as they surrounded the boat. Grayce now felt protected. The magical dance went on for hours. It was all consuming and calming. Her heart gently expanded with the mesmerizing presence of pure love. She felt a wave of ease flow through her body and she knew her angels had arrived.

Ever since Grayce could remember, she felt angels surrounded her. Grayce's vivid imagination created beautiful, helping angels that were always there listening. Grayce believed they communicated with her in her dreams. This was just a natural gift she treasured. She was also certain her mother, Frances, was an angel. Occasionally, she would appear as a soft white light gracefully hovering above young Grayce's bed. It was a sight Grayce always embraced, even though no ever told her about the presence of angels. It was something Grayce just elected to count on in life. Certainly human beings were both, unpredictable and unreliable. Unfortunately, all the people that mattered to Grayce had passed away. Believing her family were now angels helped heal the sadness in her heart. This was simply her innocence coping with the insurmountable grief. Sadly, as all humans do, she frequently doubted her angel's presence, too.

Time passes, the wind blows and sailing becomes her. Just off the bow, she saw several large schools of Mahi Mahi. This was one of her favorite fish due to their bright iridescent blue and green bodies. Grayce recalled how she secretly hated fishing because of all the times Winston and Angus took her out to murder the fish. The part when the fish is hauled out of the water and is thrown onto the boat floor would make her cry. As soon as the fish hits the air the awesome color she loved would turn a nasty gray. Then the poor fish dies. That is why she became a vegetarian. Grayce gave a little chuckle at a wicked thought; "dumb men. Sailing is superior to fishing." She amused herself with the silly insights.

As the vast sky began to be colored by the vivid sunset, several humpbacks breached in the distance. The whales were a sign of peace in the water. She loved knowing the gentle giants were swimming around her now. Grayce embraced the protection of the sea and lost herself further in the rhythm of the waves passing by the boat. She admired the ocean, appreciated the marine life and thanked God for her faithful companion, Ranger. Life was pretty good today she thought. Sailing is my peace and she smiled.

## Chapter Five

# THE ANGEL LUCA

All of a sudden, Grayce felt her boat go over something! She certainly was shocked into a state of massive alert. What could she have possibly run over? Especially, just off the coast where she had been sailing so many times before? She knew she had already passed the coral reef beds and entered into deeper waters. Then almost as fast as she felt the hit, she felt the *Silent Partner* right itself and begin to sail again. She quickly noticed a small wooden dingy float by. She was stunned, had she just ran into another boat? All these years sailing and she had never done that before. She came about in her boat and turned into the wind along side of the tiny dingy to study what had just happened.

As she neared the old tattered wood boat she saw a young boy sleeping in the bottom of the dingy. Oh no, she thought, this is not how I want to start my journey. I pray he is all right. Grayce sailed right up along the dingy and threw a line over to catch the small boat. As she did the boy jumped up, grabbed the rope and started to giggle. Ranger just stared at the little boy. Grayce became very mad and started to yell loudly at the boy; "What in the world are you doing out this far and why are you not watching for other boats? Are you hurt?"

The boy shyly replied, "Hello Grayce, my name is Luca and I am one of your guardian angels." Grayce almost fell off her boat in disbelief. Then she realized that Ranger had never even begun to bark at Luca. That was highly unusual because Ranger normally barked at everything. Luca sprang onto the *Silent Partner* like a little ballerina and tossed Grayce's line right back to her. He said, "You had better keep this line. You will be needing it later." Grayce could not even speak as she watched the tiny, tattered looking dingy float away in the warm ocean current.

Luca said, "Do not worry Grayce, I will not stay forever. Nor will I be a burden to you. I am only here to show you a few things about yourself you need to learn." Luca sauntered by her and perched himself right up front with Ranger. Without hesitation, Grayce decided to just get back to sailing. What choice was there now? She had told everyone she believed in angels. Now there was one with her right here on the boat. "Maybe if I just keep sailing he will go away," she thought to herself. Then she almost passed out when Luca said, "I am not going anywhere today Grayce, so you might as well get used to me for now."

"Grayce please do not be afraid of me. I am your friend and you can trust me. Over time you will I promise." Grayce smiled. "I am here to assist you in finding balance in the rhythm of life. I want to show you some things to help you on your journey. Experience shows me that reflection and contemplation are my allies. You have shut out most of your childhood memories because many of them caused you pain. You do not like contemplating anything. You just live as if there are no consequences. This can cause you great danger. You need to learn about discernment. Life is supposed to be fun I want you to remember this. I have traveled down many roads in my life. I have not always known exactly where I was going. Only then to be arriving at the exact place I am meant to be. Grayce, this is real. I am the angel Luca. This is truly who I am. Today, I am simply here for you." He just smiled in delight like he knew it all.

She felt a little inadequate with herself but forced herself to rally. "Honestly I have doubted my angels. Wow, I am really ashamed about that now. I just cannot believe you are real. And, I must learn to quit self analyzing and trust my divine guidance. When I hit your dingy, I instantly affirmed that I had ruined my entire journey. The situation felt catastrophic and torturous to my mind. In a split second I had ruled out any possible good outcome for myself. Mistakes feel brutal to me. They cause me to self loathe. I despise being wrong, stupid or lazy. I hate lack of confidence it is counter productive." She wanted to cry but listened instead. She judged quietly, that certainty was not something she currently possessed.

Luca responded, **"Dear Grayce, you are a jewel of unknown value. No one else can be you. As I am who I am. You are who you are. There is tremendous value in who you are. You have great family genes. You have many guiding angels. Your destiny is unfolding perfectly. Every move you make is a perfect choice. You will meet your angels and they will inspire you with life stories. In innocence and in painful growth there is always a chance for rebirth. You are a divine creation born to inspire. Your name Grayce is a sign for you that beauty is your birthright. Together, we will explore what beauty really means."**

Luca explained to Grayce what she could expect from her visiting angels. "The first family angel that will be arriving soon is your mother. Frances was a stunning woman with great strength and a regal elegance. She knew how to use her beauty as a tool for getting what she wanted. Using beauty, however, can be much stronger when used in helping others get what they want instead. In helping others, you remove the false sense of being accepted that fills your ego mind when people are admiring fading beauty."

"While it is temporarily satisfying to gain the attention of others, it is most often short lived. Compulsion to feeling admired is most unhealthy as you unknowingly grow ever more dependent upon it. Stunning looks fade and people will turn their attention elsewhere. Then a feeling of immense rejection may settle within. Timeless beauty will never fail you if it comes honestly from inside you. Confidence soars when your beauty actually comes from self-love. Grayce, my sweet mother loved to read. She introduced me to poetry. This was her favorite quote by a 13th century poet named Rumi."

***"Be melting snow, wash yourself of yourself." Rumi***

"A confident woman is a source of great strength that others may draw upon. Families thrive when the women are strong. When a woman accepts she is a divine light and her beauty radiates from within, her capabilities are limitless. A self-fulfilled woman is endlessly creative, infinitely abundant and truly inspired. This is your future, Grayce. Your mother will show you the way. She is the perfect guiding angel for you."

"Luca, my mother died when I was so young, I honestly do not remember her at all. My Dad always told me horrible stories about how selfish she was. I never even was allowed to display any photos of her in my room. The only time I was exposed to an image of her was on Grandpa's boat. I wish I knew her. I wish I had more time with her. I wish I knew what she liked. I wish I knew what she smelled like. I used to be mad at her for not being here. Then I selfishly blamed her for my problems and fears."

"Even worse, I blamed her for my fathers ongoing problem's and thought she killed him somehow. Eventually, I just got tired of being bitter towards her. But I never opened my heart to her, which I now regret. Somewhere deep inside I always knew I loved her. The love was always just buried under enormous pain. I know she has visited me in my dreams. I also feel certain she was sometimes in my room. Sadly, hovering in the dark silence. Stupidly, I never asked her to stay. Somehow I honestly knew she felt was unwelcome there."

Luca consoled, "Consider another thought from your new friend Rumi."

***"If you are irritated by the slightest rub, how will your mirror ever get polished?" Rumi***

"Regret is useless, Grayce, forget it. Focus only on right here, right now. We all want what is best for you dear, Grayce. We are here to expose you to the amazing inner blessings you possess. They are as vast as the ocean. You have just forgotten these simple truths. Everyone forgets and everyone will eventually remember. We all see the light you shine outwardly. It is very, very bright. We have watched you bravely accept all of the tragic loss in your life with innocence and determination. It makes us smile to see you face these dreadful obstacles with faith and courage. There is, however, a much easier way."

"We know the void you have felt regarding the perceived story of what happiness means. Being happy is poorly understood by most people in the world. Fortunately, we want more for you dear Grayce. We wish for you a firm knowing and a sincere expectation that everything is divinely orchestrated with you as the musician on this journey. How good would it feel to know everything will always work out for the best? We are collectively committed to helping you discover this great truth about yourself."

"Why, Luca? I was so determined to survive alone!" Realizing she was now brazenly taking an angel to task, she smiled. Luca sweetly grinned right back at her. It occurred to her she had a little bit more of Winston in her than she previously knew. She wondered what Ranger thought about it all and noticed he was sleeping. Clouds gently rolled across the sky. A warm tropical breeze guided the boat, almost effortlessly. It felt like she was in a protected cove instead of the open sea. She almost sensed it was shallow water but knew that was impossible. "Why, Luca? How is this happening?"

"This is precisely why we decided to intervene. Your confusion and anxiety does not serve you. Your journey does not have to be only about single handed survival. We want you to enjoy your life. We want you to understand your divine power. We want you to understand that by awakening your spirit, your greatness will manifest itself. Your perfectly unique contribution to the world. We love your plans for this solo sailing journey. We all decided that it was the exact time for our visits. Your days on the sea will transcend into an opportunity of growth benefiting you in many more ways than physical and individual accomplishment."

"We wish for you a total understanding of your perfection. We desire you to meet the true essence of pure love that is inside of you. The human spirit is stronger than anything else in the physical world. We wish for you to internalize this magnificent truth. Your mother wants to help you find your inner light of strength and beauty. By coming to you in her angel form these lessons are profoundly more effective, than if she were simply physically showing you. Your willingness to release her from your anger will open the door for her arrival. Are you ready for this divine invitation, Grayce?"

"Yes, Luca, surprisingly, I am more than ready. I have waited my whole life for this moment. I just never knew it would actually come. Thank you for the chance, Luca."

"Well, then, we will wait for Frances to join us. You might as well focus now on sailing, Grayce. It is quite a long way to Great Abaco."

"Luca, how did you know about Great Abaco?"

"I know everything, Grayce. I am a divine spirit and there is nothing I do not know."

"That is so amazing and awesome, Luca. I look at you and see a hungry little boy in torn, dirty clothing. You look like you could not know much at all. If you know everything, why did you fall asleep in your dingy? You risked missing me. You risked getting me killed with your stupid decision to sleep on the open sea. That certainly does not seem like an act of an all knowing divine spirit."

"That is such a funny assumption, Grayce. You give a very predictable response. Grayce, has it not occurred to you sweet child, that I knew your boat's exact course? That I fell asleep there on purpose? As for my appearance, I was a little Italian boy from Portofino, Italy at the time of my death. This is an angel assignment for me, dear Grayce. When I say, I know you must trust me. After several lifetimes of memorable and spiritual awakenings I finally accepted my true divinity. In that moment of total acceptance, surrender and obedience my souls experience was changed forever."

"When I accepted my truth I was only twelve years old. My human existence, as I knew it, was then finished. As a soul my physical identity no longer matters. In my visits with you, I command my last physical appearance in order for you to easier receive me. Plus, people tend to pass out upon seeing a real angel, wings and all. In the interest of your beloved Ranger and this special sailboat, *Silent Partner*, I thought fainting on the open sea, too big a risk to cause you to take."

"How did you did you die, Luca? Weren't your parents sad?"

"I got caught in an intense sudden ocean storm in Italy and my small dingy was capsized. The waves were immense. The water was frigid.

I invited death by drowning at sea. Yes, my parents were incredibly sad following my unexpected death. Unfortunately, there was nothing about their experience I could control. I have visited them in their dreams. They have found peace with it all now. They have realized quite on their own, that the more they drank from the infinitely deep well of love, the grief would simply go away."

Luca continued, "The pain of loss is always overshadowed by the joy of remembering. The greatest truth lies buried deep inside your heart. Those who choose to free up the wellspring of infinite love suffer no more. Grief and sorrow collapse in the presence of love and joy. Then we learn to connect with our love ones through our hearts. Grayce, you know my mother found solace in Rumi. His timeless poems helped move her through grief. Maybe his words will help you too. Open your heart to him."

*"Don't grieve.*
*Anything you lose will come around again in another form.*
*Knock and He'll open the door.*
*Vanish, and He'll make you shine like the sun.*
*Fall, and He'll raise you to the Heavens.*
*Become nothing, and He'll turn you into everything."* Rumi

The sun now setting, Grayce knew it was time for food. She asked, "Luca do you eat food?" He just chuckled, "No, Grayce but thank you. What a sweet one you are. Actually, Grayce, I am leaving for now. There is something I must supervise elsewhere. You can trust I will be back soon. Good sailing to you and Ranger. Always remember you are infinitely protected. Know I will meet up with you near Great Abaco." Without saying good bye, Luca was simply gone. She did not even see him go. He just disappeared. Grayce had to wonder if this was all just a crazy ocean mirage experience. Is it possible that she had already lost her mind so soon into her journey?

Grayce chose to check the weather on her I-pad and discovered two days had gone by! Quickly concluding she was crazy, seemed easier than understanding. What on earth could explain this? She opted to feed

Ranger. At least he was real. Grayce finally got herself some fruit and tofu. Then, Grayce settled down by watching the vast sunset across the peaceable ocean. The innocent love Grayce held for the ocean expanded. She noticed the clouds began to take shape in the image of her mother. Now what? Is this real?

For the first time, Grayce realized when thoughts about her mother came and went there was no more anger. Did Luca remove her resentments? Was that even possible? Or had she done it on her own? Where did the two days go? So many unanswered questions! Grayce decided it was just too exhausting to answer them all. Her head felt like a marble in a steel pinball machine. Unyielding determination insisted she remain focused on sailing, Ranger, and reaching Great Abaco.

*Another day turned into another night. The presence that is all things gently rolled across the vast sea like a blanket. The night sky intensely lit up by the full moon revealed the majestic green plankton floating by. There is limitless magic on the sea. Those who trust in the Creator reap untold benefits. She noticed it was 4:02 am and felt a peace she had never known before. Ranger slept like a baby and the Silent Partner practically sailed itself.*

## Chapter Six

# THE ANGEL FRANCES

The next morning the *Silent Partner* was in the midst of a large pod of once critically endangered humpback whales. Ranger watching from up front, Grayce filmed the amazing sight of these peaceable mammals all around her. She basked in the supreme feeling the whales freely shared with her. She contemplated how whales could erase memories about the unthinkable horrors of barbaric whaling that once ruled their ocean home. Could a whale actually forgive? They obviously do because people swim with them without fear. The assaulting thoughts led her no where. This new day, however, brought a new sensation. One she had not ever really felt before. A huge desire to swim with these whales overcame her. She silently pondered the logistics of doing it.

The wind was pretty fair. There was a light and steady breeze around ten knots. The calm sea would quite possibly allow her to consider the crazy idea if she decided to act. She realized the dangerous safety issues. Grayce quickly ruled against jumping overboard while sailing. She had done this countless times before in the marina at Key West. But in the middle of the open sea? No! She absolutely knew better. She promised Ranger the next chain of islands spotted, they would stop in a cove for a swim.

The whales continued to swim along side the boat for days. Grayce felt the sensation of being a part of a loving family. A warm feeling ran throughout her body. She noticed many more thoughts about love. The whales swam in divine grace. Their loving aura simply fills everything it it's presence. She wondered about her mother, Frances, and started to cry. How could my Mom have died so young? Did she love me? Was it my fault she died? Did her life have to be sacrificed for me to live alone in this world? Where is my family now? She felt sad but also a new happiness was in her heart. She curiously chewed over when Frances would show up for her visit. Grayce then saw something she was not expecting, an Albatross flying right beside the boat. What an odd place to see an Albatross, she thought.

What a magnificent bird. Grayce wondered where the beautiful creature came from. The wingspan was fantastic over ten feet. She knew that Albatross's generally do not fly in the Gulf of Mexico. Affirming it was a sign from her mother Grayce named the great bird, Frances. She watched the ease with which the large bird glided over the sea. Skimming the water with the utmost perfection. So regal, Grayce felt she was watching an elite dancer. The athleticism with which the bird navigated the wind amazed her. Relaxing now, her sailing seemed effortless. This all created a state of pure happiness and just being. Grayce knew she had fallen in love with the Albatross. Time escaped her once again and the clear morning gently gave way to night. She did not see the Albatross again.

The sighting of the first chain of islands lifted her spirits. Grayce thanked Ranger for his help navigating to the Bahamas. She pulled out her maps, turned on her depth finder and started to assess her exact location. She also pulled up Wikipedia on her I-pad. Grayce determined she was going to educate herself on all the cultures she might visit. Quite a classroom, she laughed to herself, the classroom of the world. When she turned on the I-pad she realized the date was back to normal. Had she made up the idea that two days had disappeared during her visit from Luca? No matter, she decided. Luca was probably just a crazy sailor's dream, surely everyone who sails the globe has them. Way easier to write it off as unreal than to believe it had really happened.

Excitement fuels us all. Grayce was able to easily navigate the *Silent Partner* into a small bay on one of the first islands she saw. Time for a

*the Eye*

swim, she told Ranger. She tossed the anchor in the warm water and it splashed Ranger good. They both jumped into the crystal blue water. The coral reefs were thankfully healthy. The brightly colored reef fish were abundant. Grayce and Ranger totally lost themselves in the delight of being, both off the boat and in the water. As Grayce came up for air, she noticed the Albatross flying overhead again. What a curious bird, she thought. It shocked her silly when it landed right on the boat. She instantly prayed it would not hurt itself.

Ranger had oddly gotten out of the water and was now rolling joyously in the hot sand. As she watched, the majestic Albatross took flight again and landed in the water right beside her! Silently, Grayce studied the amazing face of the intelligent bird. She was completely taken in by the beauty of the great birds' body markings. The intense face and intricate wings looked airbrushed. Supremely exquisite with fine detail. A wonder of creation. Grayce wished she could touch it but knew that would be wrong. Some of God's gifts are just too precious to do anything with, except to be revered by a state of awe.

**Silence filled the mystical moment where no thought was required.**

Grayce chose to dive under the water to look at the impressively royal bird from below. She took a long, deep breath and dove down. The water was totally clear and beautiful. She saw the glorious bird floating above her and gazed upon the impressive webbed feet. Grayce completely lost herself in admiring the bird and simultaneously soaking up the healing ocean water. She held her breath as long as she could and returned to the surface for air. Popping above the water, she quickly looked for her boat. Squinting the salt water out of her eyes, Grayce saw a woman sitting on the boat. How could that be? She looked again and realized it was her mother, Frances. Just sitting right there on the boat like she had always been there.

Grayce knew she had lost her mind now and began to hyperventilate. Time simply stopped, again. Frances dove into the water, easily grabbing Grayce. Holding her like a new born baby. Fear vanished and Grayce felt like an infant. In a split second, Grayce remembered everything about this woman. What she felt the most was the overpowering feeling of being loved unconditionally. She slowed her breathing and closed her eyes. Her heartbeat calmed down and she was completely immersed in the surreal fantasy. She felt Frances's heartbeat align with her own. Grayce figured there was more happening than she might be able to even understand.

Grayce opened her eyes, now magically back on the *Silent Partner.* Sitting ever so calmly, right there with her was Frances. "Grayce, I love you more than you know. Have trust in it all. Please just suspend your fears. Yes, angels are real. And, yes I am one. Luca told you I was coming, so hopefully you were expecting me." Grayce could not find any words. She just studied the beauty of Frances's unchanged youthful face. They just smiled at each other and at the Albatross too, who was now back on the boat.

"Grayce, I know this is all very hard for you to accept. That is ok. We learn the most when it is scary. Do not fight it though, just relax. There are infinite portals to divine gifts if your heart is open enough to receive the experience being offered. I have been trying to reach you for years, but your heart was just closed off. You might remember dreams of my visiting your room when you were a little girl. Those memories are real. It is just your conscious mind would not allow for you to accept me as reality. Luca simply opened the door for you. Now I know you are finally ready to fully accept my love. My desire is to show you your divine grace and help you see your inner beauty."

Grayce was crying now. Fumbling around in her mind for words. She was trying to understand how this could happen. The more she tried the harder it was to see. "Grayce if you would just believe and quit fighting this would all be much easier. It is called walking in faith, not fear. Look at the Albatross, isn't he lovely? You accepted seeing him although this is not his flight path. Why not accept me too?" Grayce blurted out, "But, mother you are dead!" And with those sharp words, Frances disappeared. Grayce started to cry and called out for Frances to return. She then yelled at the top of her lungs and scared the Albatross way. She screamed some more obscenities and sobbed uncontrollably until she lost her voice.

Ranger immediately returned from the beach and tried to comfort her. She just crumbled down in the floor of the boat sobbing without anymore thought. Finally, exhausted she fell asleep right there on the floor of her boat. Now with soaking wet Ranger calmly resting by her side. They just lay there together, a tumbled heap of two connected souls. Two sand covered bodies, in what one might call a **surrendered and unified state of peace.**

Grayce woke up a couple of hours later and felt consumed with anger. How stupid of me to let these ridiculous distractions deter me from my sailing. She immediately pulled the anchor up and hoisted her sail. She pulled up her navigation map on her I-pad and focused on getting to Great Abaco. The sailing was fairly easy; the light winds in the Gulf of Mexico were sweet. Grayce called Ranger to sit by her side. He always had a way of calming her mind. Unfortunately, her thoughts were racing out of control. She knew it and hated herself for allowing all of this to happen.

Something deep inside nagged; ***If you are fighting an Alpha dog, and you are not an alpha dog, dear Grayce, why are you trying to be one?*** The higher level thought made her laugh. Grayce had a side of her that was dark. She battled inner demons just like everyone else. When she got mad she usually focused on other people. Grayce had terrible thoughts about her Dad. Now she was locked into wondering about his relationship with Frances. Her recent encounter with Frances had softened her attitude about her late mother. It seemed easier now to shift the usual anger she carried from her Mother to her Dad. She got lost in herself wondering if any of the rumors about her Dad were ever true? She recalled many people asking her if her Angus had been responsible for Frances's death. Was that a horrible rumor or true? The thought made her feel sick. She assumed there was simply no way of knowing.

## Chapter Seven

# PINK FLAMINGOS

Grayce firmly ruled these thoughts were taking her nowhere. She looked out over the open sea which always calmed her mind. Cruising along, she looked down by her side. Grayce noticed a book sitting on the seat cushion of the boat. Funny, she thought to herself, I do not remember this book being on my boat. Where could it have come from, she wondered? Then she realized it was the same book that was in the basket from Mrs. Poe. My mind has sure been playing tricks with me. Especially with these pestering visits from angels and all. A book though, now this is real. Strange indeed. She reluctantly admitted she could not deny the book's moving out of the basket on its own. She opened it to a short story and a picture of Frances fell out. The story by Kahlil Gibran read:

*The River*

*In the valley of Kadisha where the mighty river flows, two little streams met and spoke to one another. One stream said, "How came you my friend, and how was your path?"*
*And, the other answered, "My path was most encumbered. The wheel of the mill was broken, and the master farmer who used to conduct me from my channel to his plants, is*

*dead. I struggled down oozing with the filth of those who do naught but sit back and bake their laziness in the sun. But how was your path, my brother?"*

*And the other stream answered and said, "Mine was a different path. I came down the hill among the fragrant flowers and shy willows, men and women drank of me with silvery cups, and little children paddled their rosy feet at my edges, and there was a laughter all about me, and there were sweet songs. What a pity that your path was not so happy."*

*At that moment the river spoke with a loud voice and said, "Come in, come in, we are going to the sea. Come in, come in, speak no more. Be with me now. We are going to the sea. Come in, come in, for in me you shall forget your wanderings, sad or gay. Come in, come in. And you and I will forget all our ways when we reach the heart of our mother sea." Kahlil Gibran*

Grayce was smart enough to consider the story and think about the meaning. It did not dawn on her why it had fallen out of the basket yet. She even fully refused to contemplate the picture of Frances. Her thoughts vacillated between, I might like this silly book and then again I might elect to throw it over board. She humored herself with her ridiculous mind and lack of temperance with regards to these assaulting, annoying thoughts. For a girl who fought any type of serious love in her life, it sure was showing up in the form of this somewhat agitating book right now.

The book felt good in her hand she hated to admit. It was a small black book with a single red heart on the cover. The book cover made her think of Valentine's Day. All that did was remind her what a stupid holiday that was. A whole world stops for the day, then over spends money on useless gifts, all in the name of love. It kind of made her feel kind of sick. No one ever gave me anything on Valentine's Day, not even once. What a ridiculous occasion, full of chocolate, candy and hearts, who needs that? She smiled and laughed at herself.

*the Eye*

Grayce put the mysteriously mobile book back down below. She decided to look at it again when she was bored. Best leaving that book of love alone for now, she proudly thought. She eyed the gift basket for a moment recalling how sweet it was when Mrs. Poe had given it to her all filled with fresh baked goodies. Now it was all empty and filling up with smelly, dirty rags instead. Love, what a silly waste of time. Who needs it anyway? I have Ranger! That is all the love I will ever need.

A large flock of Pink Flamingo's started flying along side the *Silent Partner*. Grayce watched them for hours amazed by their grace and unity. Animals seem to possess a natural ability to trust each other. They know not to fly in each other's space. The wind works easily for all of them, not just a few. They do not question, they just fly. And, their instincts teach them all they need to know. It's really magic. How do they do it? Why do they not crash into each other? What are they accessing to be so powerful? And, how is something so beautiful and delicate so strong? Grayce allowed the questions to just roll around in her mind. She had no easy answers for anything.

She took some photos and posted them onto her Facebook page. The Flamingos continued to fly with her for over four hours. It was unlike anything she had ever seen before. She found herself silently communicating with them. There were questions as to why but she decided it was better to not try and understand. Nature gives us many surprises. The pretty ones gift us joy. Grayce concluded the Flamingos brought her happiness. That was all she needed today. Love is for other people I am doing just fine by myself. She winked at Ranger. Grayce definitely felt a bit insincere about declaring to be so brave. She knew this sail would not have happened without Ranger. He was her rock of strength. She gave thanks, realized she was exhausted and sighed.

## Chapter Eight

# GREAT ABACO

Two days later Grayce and Ranger arrived at Great Abaco. The stunningly beautiful island was just as she imagined it would be. Dotted with countless palm trees and covered in white sandy beaches. It was perfect. She navigated her way into the small marina and found an empty slip. There were quite a few people walking around the docks but no one noticed Grayce. She let down her sails and went about tidying up the boat. She was happy the sailing had been successful and predictable so far. Except of course, for the sightings of two angels and the mysterious Albatross. Grayce wondered when she would run into Luca. She decided to focus on finding the Spanish Barb horses of Great Abaco.

Assuredly, Grayce asked around the docks inquiring if anyone knew about the horses. She saw a tall and very tanned young man approaching her. She asked him about the horses. He suggested she go see, Mrs. Heartworth, who owned a local bakery. The man explained, "Her son, Josh is quite involved with the wild horses. Mrs. Heartworth is a respected business woman and everyone adores her. I think you will find her easily approachable and very kind. Best pastries on the island too." Grayce asked him where her bakery was and he gave her the directions. It is called the *Bakery from the Heart*. Grayce was instantly drawn to this name and figured she was going to love Mrs. Heartworth.

Grayce and Ranger made their way downtown to the *Bakery from the Heart*. The directions from the tall man were easy. Grayce thought the bakery was precious at first sight. The sign out front was a large heart hand painted in bright tropical colors. There were adorable wooden boxes in the front window full of bright colored flowers. She could smell the baked treats even before she walked inside. As she approached the bakery she thought about Mrs. Poe and how lucky she was to now meet another fine woman who cooked. Her stomach started to rumble a little. Grayce realized she was exceptionally hungry. There was a place to tie up Ranger out front with a beautiful, hand painted bowl and fresh water. Looking into the bottom of water dish she noticed a small red heart. She chuckled and realized this love thing was simply not going to let her go.

As she entered the bakery she saw a tall beautiful woman with a pink apron singing and putting something in the oven. Grayce hoped this was Mrs. Heartworth and went ahead introducing herself. Mrs. Heartworth had a fabulous smile and instantly dropped what she was doing to meet Grayce. "What a delight to meet you, Grayce. Thank you for coming to my bakery." Grayce's heart melted and her stomach growled again. "It is my pleasure to meet you too, Mrs. Heartworth. And, I hear you have a son named Josh. I am seeking out the wild Spanish Barb horses here on Great Abaco. I was told Josh works with the horses."

"Why yes, Josh works with the horses everyday. Josh is about your age Grayce. I will certainly enjoy introducing the two of you. Everyone tells me he is a total knock out. Josh has coal black hair and green eyes. I think he is precious, but I am expectedly a bit partial to my son. He cherishes horses. No, Josh is absolutely crazy about horses!" Grayce was admiring the lovely woman and looking around at her beautiful bakery. "Are you thirsty Grayce? Hungry?" Grayce's eyes lit up and Mrs. Heartworth went about pouring her a big, cool glass of lemonade. There was a slice of lemon and mint leaves floating in the glass. "Never turn away home made goodies with fresh lemonade, never. I offer with love from me to you." Grayce agreed, "Thank you Mrs. Heartworth."

There was a beautiful assorted plate of fresh baked cookies and the prettiest croissant Grayce had ever seen. Grayce noticed that Mrs. Heartworth had taken the time to lovingly place three lovely flowers on the plate. She even placed a beautiful linen placemat under the plate. What a difference the beauty made in the presentation. She imagined someday she might do these nice things. She then realized she had never even owned or used a placemat. Shameful about my tomboy ways, thinking to herself. Grayce then fully turned her attention towards eating.

Grayce wasted no time devouring the food in front of her and washed it all down with the refreshing lemonade. Mrs. Heartworth watched in amazement, silently wondering when the last time the thin girl had a good meal. She asked Grayce about Ranger, "Is he hungry too?" Grayce smiled, "Oh you can bet he is." Mrs. Heartworth produced a large soup bone from the well-stocked fridge and asked Grayce if Ranger liked bones. "Oh yes, he loves them." Grayce popped up from her chair and quickly took the bone out to Ranger who had been watching everything from the window. Sitting calmly, wagging his tail and waiting with great patience for his turn at a delicious meal. When she returned, Grayce's plate was full again with more baked goodies, fresh flowers. She smiled and gave thanks for kind people.

Mrs. Heartworth asked Grayce how it was she had decided to sail around the world all by herself. "My dream is to discover many cultures and find out what makes each one uniquely different. Sadly, my family is all gone. I truly just want to learn more about the planet. I grew up sailing with my Grandfather and I could not afford to fly. It seemed that by sailing around the world, I might be lucky enough to discover what I wanted to do with my life. There is really nothing to tie me to where I grew up, so I embraced the idea of seeing the world by sailboat. My Grandfather had restored my sailboat, *Silent Partner* and in many ways when I am sailing I feel we are still together."

Mrs. Heartworth got a little teary eyed and smiled. "What a beautiful dream dear Grayce, it is truly courageous. Are you not worried about safety and being a girl, all alone at sea for so long?" Grayce grinned, "Fear is simply not something I allow in my sailing. My Grandfather taught me all about navigating the ocean and understanding the weather. Besides, I have Ranger to protect me." Grayce noticed Ranger wagged his tail from outside, as if he knew exactly what was being said. "Well, I insist you stay with me for a few days until you are thoroughly rested before you resume your journey. Ranger is welcome too. I absolutely insist." Grayce was not sure how to process such a lovely gesture.

"Grayce, I have a big house with plenty of extra rooms. This way you can also meet Josh and spend some time with the horses." Grayce shocked herself by going right over and giving Mrs. Heartworth a big hug. "Thank you so much. I am so happy we have met. It is such a wonderful opportunity for me to see Great Abaco. Yes, I am thrilled to accept your very sweet offer!" Grayce was amazed she had met someone so quickly. Suddenly feeling quite relieved she would be able to sleep a couple of nights in a real bed. Grayce quickly decided not to post that part online, it might look like cheating or reflect weakness. Then she laughed remembering this was not a contest and there were no rules. She giggled inside thinking about how many people, including Winston and Angus, might think she was becoming soft. Grayce knew nothing about luxury. Most of her life has been on boats, certainly not in beautiful homes. The draw to Mrs. Heartworth was not the cottage, but rather her love.

## Chapter Nine

# THE BOY

Just then a very attractive, tall boy walked in the bakery. Grayce guessed this was Josh and by the way he hugged Mrs. Heartworth, she knew she was right. Grayce had not expected a boy so incredibly good looking. She could not help staring at Josh. Her heart felt like it was working overtime. She felt it beating like a bass drum. She actually wondered if they could hear it. Grayce tried to hide her excitement but knew she could not. Mrs. Heartworth made the introduction, "Josh, I would like for you to meet Grayce. She as sailed here from Key West all by herself. Grayce is on quite an epic journey, sailing solo around the world! Can you believe that? She stopped here on Great Abaco to meet the Spanish Barb horses. I told her you could help her with this."

Josh smiled and gave Grayce a big, bear hug. She almost passed out right there in the bakery. "Hello Grayce. It is great to meet you. I saw your sailboat down at the dock and wondered who it belonged to. Cool name on your boat, *Silent Partner*, I like it. Yeah sure, I would really dig taking you to see the horses. It is quite a little drive though, how much time do you have?" Grayce responded quickly, "I have as much time as it takes." She thought to herself, Josh as cute as you are, I hope it takes days. She giggled a little and smiled. "I am setting my own schedule so I can be a little flexible." Josh sat down. Mrs. Heartworth produced another glass of lemonade with more pastries. He wolfed down every bite. Grayce simply stared. He slowly drank the lemonade and began telling Grayce about the horse herd.

"The horses are in desperate shape. Actually, there are only five left. Down from thirty just five years ago. We have lost the important young stallion too, which makes things worse. Without his breeding ability there might not be any more babies. The question arises whether to bring an outside stud horse in, but that compromises the purity of this herd. We have evidence of DNA proving they are an original line of Spanish Barb horses. The only ones on the planet. Left alone they will become extinct within a few years, if not sooner. It is all terribly sad, but I know there is only so much I can do. I fight modern logging, which removes vital trees and destroys the horse's food and shelter. Outside buyers of wood offer more money in one season of cutting than these local people could make in ten years. That is hard to fight. Some of these horribly negative issues are overwhelming but sadly beyond my control."

Grayce looked at Josh with the saddest eyes he had ever seen. "Isn't there anything we can do? There is always hope if you look hard enough, isn't there?" Josh agreed. He added, "We also fight forest fires which are dangerous for the horses and savaging the land. The worse thing I fight is the locals who do not even like the horses. A few people have actually tried to kill them by setting some of these fires. Then they shoot at the poor horses as they flee the fire they intentionally set. It is illegal, but it does not stop them from trying. It is horrifying and has been effectively deadly. I try and watch the entire herd as best as I can. No way I can always be there for everything. It is frustrating to say the least."

Grayce was at a loss for words and a great sadness engulfed her heart. Josh lightened things up by offering to take her for a ride in his jeep. Mrs. Heartworth told them both to be very careful. She sweetly suggested Grayce gather any laundry from her boat if she needed it washed. "I am totally happy to help out with that and anything else you might need. If you need any supplies make a list and I will go into town for you too." Grayce smiled and thought about the dirty rags in the gift basket from Mrs. Poe. "Thank you Mrs. Heartworth. Yes, that is a big help. You are an amazing woman Josh is lucky to have you as a mother." Mrs. Heartworth tossed back her hair a little and flashed a great smile. "Yes, I know. Thank you for noticing. Grayce, I love being a mother." They hugged and Mrs. Heartworth gave her a business card with her phone number on it. "You never know when you might need this, please keep it safe." Tears rolled down Grayce's face and said, "Bless you Mrs. Heartworth." Grayce grabbed her backpack and Ranger. They all headed out to Josh's blue jeep parked out front.

Josh's jeep was a disaster and he tried to make room for Grayce by throwing everything in back. Poor Ranger was crammed in between a surfboard, a kite board and some extra gear bags too. Grayce asked what was in the bags and Josh told her he loved photography. My Mom has bought me some really nice cameras. I love shooting pictures of everything. Grayce, I even took a few photos of your sailboat. I will show you later if you like. She replied, "Yeah sure that would be cool, thanks." Grayce wondered what could possibly be interesting about her boat? Then decided not to waste any energy thinking about that. Grayce then became oddly distracted by the girl's sandals she saw on the floor of the jeep, but said nothing. She noticed she felt both jealous and angry by the sight of the harmless shoes.

Never mind, she thought to herself. Of course, it went on as she scolded herself harshly. She insisted inside, do not be ridiculous you just met him. Let it go Grayce. Amused by her mind chatter, she asked, "How far are the horses Josh?" He put on his black Ray Bans and replied, "About thirty minutes from here. It is an awesome drive though and you will enjoy it. I will take you along the beach access road and the views are perfect. I grew up here on Great Abaco and I still can stare at the ocean all day long." Grayce agreed, "I know what you mean. Growing up in Key West, I was on the water everyday. The ocean is something I must be a part of to feel complete. The water calms me, removes any fears or doubts I have about anything and reminds me what is important in life." He looked and her and said, "Ditto!"

Josh asked about Grayce's family and she told them they were all gone. "My grandfather raised me after both my parents were killed. He was a wonderful man. I miss him terribly. His name was Winston Kingsley. He taught me about sailing and the ocean. Then eventually he died too. I am all alone now. That is why I am sailing around the world solo." Josh didn't really know what to say. There was a silence among them for a time but neither one seemed to mind.

Josh pointed out all his favorite surfing spots and they got out at one for a swim. Ranger was the first one in the water and made them laugh. Grayce played fetch with him and showed Josh what an amazing retriever he was. They enjoyed the sand and the sun a while. A feeling of happiness perfumed the air. Now it was time to move on and go see the horses. Grayce watched Josh as he drove. She could not help admire how cute he was. Grayce had not had a boyfriend yet, always having been too busy with Winston and sailing. She briefly wondered about love and quickly tossed that thought aside, reminding herself that was not for her.

As they drove along the beach, Grayce was shocked to see a familiar boy along the side of the road. It was Luca! Standing right there on the side of the road in his little tattered shorts and dirty white shirt. Luca looked exactly like he did last time. She wondered if Josh could see him. When he drove right by without a word she knew he could not. Turning around to see if she was dreaming, Luca was still back there all right. Grinning ear to ear and waving at her like someone in a parade. Grayce knew better than to try and explain Luca to Josh, so she kept it to herself. Ranger was looking too and wagging his tail. Grayce wondered if Ranger saw Luca too. Grayce could not believe Luca had come to Great Abaco. Exactly as he said he would do. She thought to herself about his presence and decided it must be a dream. Maybe I have had too much sun she thought. Deep in her heart, Grayce definitely hoped Luca was real.

## Chapter Ten

# HORSES OF GREAT ABACO

Josh said they were nearing the Great Abaco Wild Horse Preserve and started to explain to Grayce a little more about the history of the horses. "Grayce, just imagine many years ago when an impressive sailing ship carrying a sophisticated Spanish family and thirty of their fine Spanish Barb horses, tragically met with disaster. A level five hurricane hit Great Abaco and destroyed everything in its path. The ship was called the *Flying Pegasus* and it was a massive sailing ship with nine sails. The family name was Magneto and they were obviously entitled royalty from Spain."

"The Magneto's enjoyed great fame for their supreme line of well-bred and extremely talented horses. They supplied all of the horses to the Spanish monarchy. The King of Spain loved the Magneto's horses. This tragic and fateful trip the entire family was on board. Thirty-two people including women, children and grandparents. There were also a few well known global explorers on board. They had also brought many of their beloved purebred horses. The Magneto's had previously settled on three different islands in the Caribbean. That all happened during the Spanish Colonization of the Bahamas. This tremendous storm took the Magneto family quite by surprise. The hurricane came on suddenly in the black of night. A rouge wave, reportedly capsized the mighty vessel. The entire family and horses were all thrown into the raging sea. Sadly, all but three members of the family drowned that dreadful night. Amazingly, all of the beautiful horses survived."

"Oh Josh, that is the saddest story I have ever heard. Is that how the horses arrived on Great Abaco?" She felt so sad all of a sudden. "Yes, Grayce it is. And, there are still three descendants of the Magneto's still living on Great Abaco today. They have desperately tried to preserve this heritage of Spanish Barb horses too. It is a shame because not many people seem to care very much about the horses. They may say they want to help but when it comes to offering money or time their commitment wavers. The herd is down to just five horses left. It is my mission to help them the best way I know how. I am trying to preserve a critically endangered species too. Many battles are unequal I know that. This one is tragically leaning against any odds given for the horse's chances of survival. Still, I won't give up."

"Grayce, as I told you before deforestation has been the primary enemy. Without the protection of trees, the horses will not make it here anymore. The trees provide both shelter and food. Without the trees the horses are threatened, exposed and starving. Dog attacks are another brutal experience the horses have suffered. Many of the locals do nothing to stop it. Some just coldly turn their backs. There are three mares within the preserve. The two stallions are unfortunately running wild outside of the preserve."

"We simply cannot track the stallions. It is just too expensive and hard. We would need a better tractor. The one I drive is broken all the time with no money to fix it. The horses do have names. The mares are Alcamar, Alnitak, and Nunki. The two stallions are Hadar and Capella. The mares stay inside the preserve on the farm. We can feed them to ensure they maintain proper weight. Grayce, the breed is almost extinct and that is permanent." Josh stopped the jeep at an old rustic gate and got out to open it. As tears rolled down her face, Grayce tried to regain her composure. She was feeling queasy after learning the sad and tragic fate of these poor, almost certainly, extinct horses.

*the Eye*

As they drove into the farm, Grayce felt disappointed by the sad condition of things. Josh parked the jeep under a palm tree. The wire fences were all in awful shape. There was discarded junk everywhere making a real mess of things. When she saw the horses they looked pathetic, thin and hungry. They sure do not look like the show horses in Palm Beach she thought. Just then a bouncy young girl ran up and opened Josh's door. She all but jumped into his lap and started kissing him. Talk about a shift, Grayce's attention to the horses momentarily vanished.

All of a sudden Grayce felt sick and all she could think of was getting as far away from here as possible. She wondered if Josh could sense her disgust and really hoped not. She quickly felt guilty with all these intense feelings swirling but quickly settled on confused and indifferent. Josh introduced Grayce to the young girl. "Grayce this is Amanda. I appreciate the free help she gives me here on the farm with chores and feeding. She also is a surfing buddy of mine and we dig going to the ocean together." Pause, wait for it. Anger, yes it definitely exists when you least expect it.

Grayce felt like someone had kicked her in the stomach. She somehow managed a pathetically forced Princess Diana smile and reluctantly held out her hand. As Grayce politely faked her way through the impossibly uncomfortable introduction, her attention turned to one of the horses in the paddock. She could not believe what she saw. Luca was sitting on the back of the mare called Nunki! A smile came over her face and she was filled with an enormous sense of relief. Luca winked at her and then blew her a little kiss. Grayce knew that Josh and Amanda could not see Luca, which made the whole experience even more timely and sweet. She strolled over to Nunki and began petting her neck. The mare happily responded with a little nicker.

Luca whispered to Grayce, **"Remember Grayce why you are here. You did not come to find love with Josh, while that is still possible. You came to bring awareness to this issue of the horses on Great Abaco facing extinction. You wanted to learn more about the world. Ask Josh to take some pictures of the horses for you. You can spread the horse's spirit through photos wherever you so choose. Embrace** *this situation for what it is exactly. Do not become lost in your petty jealousy. That never serves you well. Focus on why you came to the island. Think of your higher goal not yourself."*

Grayce surprisingly understood everything Luca had just said and felt her angry feelings melt into gratitude. She sincerely thanked Luca. He said he would be waiting for her back at the boat. With that, he was gone. Grayce continued to pet Nunki and gave her a big kiss. She looked into her big brown eyes, promising to try and help. She looked at Josh and asked him about the photos. "Can we take some photos of the horses, Josh? I can post them on my Facebook page and blog. There are a lot of people tracking my sailing journey. It is a great platform to spread awareness about these poor horses." Josh smiled, "Very cool idea, Grayce. I will get my camera. Right on!"

Amanda was basically oblivious to everything and simply went on about doing her chores. Grayce realized that by ignoring her jealous feelings the ugly situation she had felt before just vanished. She became aware that it had all been in her mind. She opted to pick a bright red hibiscus flower then put it in Nunki's mane. It looked fabulous. This small act of kindness made her feel so happy. Grayce quietly laughed to herself. She wondered if Mrs. Heartworth had magically rubbed some womanly charm on her somehow. She smiled at Josh and said, "OK, let's take some pictures."

During the horses' little photo shoot Grayce was able to feed some grain to the three mares. It soothed her soul noticing how wonderful it felt inside while caring for something else. When the attention is on others the emotions just seem to calm down. She hoped she could carry forth this important lesson and wondered if that meant grace was smiling on her. She thought briefly about her mom and decided Frances would certainly be proud.

Josh asked her if she wanted to head out and drive to another great swimming beach. Grayce happily agreed, "Yes, Josh please." Amanda bounced over and told Grayce what a pleasure it had been to meet her. She asked to connect on Facebook so they could remain friends. The two girls hugged and smiled. Grayce wondered if she would have managed to be so kind to Amanda had it been her in the jeep with Josh. She tried to quiet her overactive mind and focus on being nice. She was no longer curious but still a little mad about the sandals in Josh's Jeep.

Grayce felt relieved she had seen the mares. It felt even better when she had been able to feed them. The horses were sad looking but they were alive. Saving a species is an impossibly hard task. Luca had smartly reminded her what her real goal on this beautiful island really was. Josh and Grayce settled to come back again tomorrow and feed the mares again. She would post her Great Abaco horse photos online and then refocus on her own sailing. The thought of getting back to sea calmed her down. Confidence returned and her mind stopped racing. Grayce was especially grateful Luca was true to his word.

For now, Grayce chose to just savor her time alone with Josh. Luca mysteriously disappeared again. Now, Grayce knew she could trust he would be back. She called for Ranger and he climbed in the back of the jeep again. They drove out the farm gate heading for the beach. Grayce looked forward to another swim with Josh. She also secretly hoped for a special dinner with Mrs. Heartworth. Grayce laughed at herself thinking that now she had met Amanda there was no more pressure about what might happen with Josh. Grayce would be glad she had met a new family to embrace and leave thoughts about possibly having a boyfriend alone. She wondered, am I gaining wisdom?

*Chapter Eleven*

# COTTAGE SANCTUARY

As they drove along the scenic coast Josh told Grayce more stories about life on Great Abaco. "My Mom moved here after she and my Dad divorced when I was about four years old. Actually, they had honeymooned on Great Abaco and that is how she first learned about the island. Mom loves Great Abaco and adores her home here. She had always dreamed of opening a bakery and the divorce provided the chance to do just that. I guess my Dad was pretty financially stable and Mom got a great settlement. I feel lucky they did not go to war it was actually pretty civil. It was enough to buy the cottage and start up the bakery."

Grace was surprised he opened up about his father and was shocked when she learned he was living in Florida. "I have never met him and I thought I knew everybody in Key West." Josh turned into a beach access road and they parked the jeep under a palm tree. Coconuts scattered the beach so they picked up a few. Grayce got Ranger out of the back and headed to the bathroom to change back into her bathing suit. She hated putting on a wet suit but decided swimming with Josh was worth a little personal hassle.

Swimming was a lot of fun for Grayce and Ranger too. Josh was so familiar with the cove and knew just where to go for the most marine life. Ranger chased waves while Grayce and Josh went snorkeling. There were many adorable green sea turtles and elegant manta rays. Grayce felt like she was in a movie, swimming in such a beautiful location with a guy as handsome as any movie star. She laughed inside. Amused with her endless self-directed story telling in the safety of her head. She also liked the idea that while swimming she did not have to speak to Josh. It was easier to hang onto her imagined movie storyline if they were not talking. This made everything seem surreal as she pretended to forget about meeting Amanda. The vast range of emotions she was experiencing were somewhat overwhelming to her but in a strange way she liked it.

The sunset was nearing and they decided it was time to call it a day. They headed back to town for dinner with Mrs. Heartworth. The joy of being alone with Josh was quickly replaced by an intense, out of place anger when Amanda unexpectedly called. Grayce could tell by the conversation that Amanda needed something. As Josh kept talking on the phone, Grayce felt herself become increasingly jealous. She hated these ridiculous feelings that were surfacing. She chose to become aloof and silent. I must not show him I care, she thought to herself. The jeep ride became extraordinarily uncomfortable and Grayce fought back tears.

As they pulled up to Mrs. Heartworth's lovely home, Josh was still trying to explain why he was going to miss dinner. Grayce was tuning him out as best as she knew how but she suspected he knew of her tremendous disappointment. Grayce was stunned when Josh all but kicked her and Ranger out in the driveway. He asked her to apologize to his Mom and said he would be back later. Grayce watched the blue jeep disappear into the night as more tears just rolled down her tanned face. She tried to pull herself together and gave Ranger a big hug. "At least you never let me down boy. I love you Ranger."

Mrs. Heartworth opened the front door and asked Grayce to come in. "I have made a shrimp and avocado salad with mango. Grayce, are you hungry my dear?" Grayce realized she was totally famished and also soaking wet. "Thank you Mrs. Heartworth. Yes, I am incredibly hungry. Could I take a shower first though?" She giggled thinking how dirty she must look. "Let's go inside and get you cleaned up Grayce.

Bring Ranger along." Walking inside the cottage a pretty needle point pillow quickly caught her eye.

> **We are the seed and the law produces the plant.**
> **Your garden blooms when you allow it.**

Walking into the kitchen, Grayce explained that Josh had to go meet Amanda. Mrs. Heartworth just shook her head from side to side. "Amanda is always needing something. I hardly see Josh anymore. It is hard to be mad at him though because they are in love." Grayce almost fell over trying to process those impossibly hard words. She felt herself becoming consumed with anger and overwhelmed by thoughts of Amanda and Josh. She hoped Mrs. Heartworth could not read her mind. Grayce felt embarrassed by the stream of images floating through her young mind. She felt anger, passion, hope, sadness, joy, laughter, and even pain. It was all so confusing!

Mrs. Heartworth showed Grayce around and then invited her to use the guesthouse to clean up. They went out back to another stone cottage covered in bright, fuchsia colored flowers. "Grayce I have fixed everything up for you. Just make yourself at home. There is an outdoor shower on the back wall of the cottage where you can bathe Ranger. You have fresh towels and a pitcher of cool lemonade inside on the counter. Mrs. Heartworth opened the hand-carved, wooden, Dutch door and showed Grayce inside. There was a feeling of coziness everywhere and it smelled like fresh flowers. The bed was simply fantastic. All decorated in blue and yellow pillows with a big, fluffy, white comforter.

As Grayce imagined a long nap on the amazing bed. She asked Mrs. Heartworth what time they would eat. "Let's have dinner in about an hour. Grayce, take your time. If you need longer that is fine." Grayce replied, "Thank you so much. I am so happy to be here with you." Mrs. Heartworth slipped out the front door and waltzed back over to the main cottage. Grayce admired her style and watched her every move until she disappeared inside. A quiet peace filled the still room. Silence. If I am ever a Mom, I want to be just like her. Grayce paused briefly. No idea where that stupid idea came from!

Looking around the cottage, Grayce noticed there were photos everywhere. The pictures were in beautiful silver frames. All shapes and sizes. She poured a glass of lemonade and began to more closely study the images. As she took a drink, Grayce saw a photo that really caught her eye. The picture had Mrs. Heartworth in it with someone else. He was a very handsome and familiar man. Grayce noticed it because it looked like they were at a horse show. Her innocent eyes instantly saw deceit. Rage consumed her innocent mind. Anger spread as fast as a match setting fire to dry timber.

Grayce dropped her glass of lemonade. It shattered glass everywhere. She had realized the man in the photo was her Dad, Angus! It was sure enough him just smiling right at her. They were at a horse show, presumably Palm Beach. Grayce suddenly thought she might throw up but had no idea where a proper lady would do that. She usually just threw up over the bow of a boat into the ocean. Luckily, Grayce decided on the bathroom and not the white down comforter still perfect on the soft bed.

Grayce had to run, far and fast, away from all of this mess. Dinner was in less than an hour and she was torn on what to do. She felt like a caged tiger pacing the floor of the soul filled guest cottage. Thoughts racing through her mind tormenting her like a savage beast. She then saw a picture of Josh, too. She felt so confused and wondered what does this now mean about Josh? Her feelings turned to rage and she just wanted to flee from the house. She was not sure how far the house was from the marina but quickly concluded it could not be that hard to find. Determination and anger fuels the best intended fires however misplaced or misguided in origin.

Raging now and fueled by irrational thoughts, Grayce resolved to leave. She grabbed her things and called for Ranger. Slowly pausing to take one last look at the dreadful picture of her youthful and obviously unfaithful Dad. The photo was old and she reluctantly admitted he looked unbelievably happy. She stuffed the photo in her backpack and headed right out the door. "I simply cannot stand facing Mrs. Heartworth," she thought sadly to herself. Guilt immediately overtook her heart as she contemplated not only stealing the photo but accidentally

*the Eye*

breaking the glass and then just leaving it on the floor. Intellect now gone, survival set in.

A split second later she opted to avoid Mrs. Heartworth altogether and then slipped out the gate into the black night. The road to town was not far. The anger she was carrying now fed her with plenty of energy. She followed the lights. It was not long before she saw a sign pointing her in the direction of the harbor. Ranger trotted alongside her as if he already knew where they were going, when it began to rain. The rain felt good on her face washing the tears away. Approaching the entrance to the harbor, Grayce saw a familiar sight, Luca! Her heart slowed down and she decided to start breathing again.

## Chapter Twelve

# THE CALM

Grayce smiled to herself as a familiar calm came over her whole being. She noted it was now 4:02 am. She had no idea what happened to the time. Luca was sitting in the rain on a small rock wall that bordered the dimly lit entry to the harbor. Her heart felt lighter and protected. She managed a smile and sweetly said, "Oh my Luca." He jumped off the wall, stood up straight and said, "Hi Grayce, let's go sailing! I know you are hurting and that is alright. This is what our friend Rumi have would to say about that."

*"The wound is where the light enters." Rumi*

She had no idea where the missing time went but decided having faith in Luca was all that mattered for now. Her heart was now savaged after Josh's rude exit earlier tonight, the mortifying photo of Angus, and her own running out on dinner with Mrs. Heartworth. Her embarrassment was now completely off the charts punishing. Grayce decided at this point, Luca was the only sane one. She knew to keep that part to herself. Luca smiled and winked at her. No more words were needed.

*Grayce now knew he heard her thoughts too. A great wave of calm came over Grayce, one she had not ever felt before. Something was actually slowing down her thoughts and her anger was disappearing. Luca smiled and touched her heart by saying, "I know, it is nice isn't it?" They continued to walk in silence down the dock to the boat. "What is this peaceful feeling taking hold of me Luca?" A moment passed and Luca simply said, "pure love." Looking perplexed as ever Grayce replied, "I don't understand. I need to be mad right now and it seems the wrong choice."*

*Luca smiled that little grin only a spiritually enlightened angel can radiate, then he waited. He paused the conversation until they reached the boat, "Grayce, you are in the Eye. It is a point of access to divine love. I am a conduit for you to feel the power of pure love, which is not ego based but rather the opposite, which is holy. You had an emotional shock back there with both Josh and the picture of Angus. You are divine. When you allow that connection to eliminate your fear, doubt, and worry a miracle will occur. I absolutely understand. We can move forward from here with forgiveness, love, trust, understanding and compassion."*

Grayce delighted in the freedom from worrying about her problems. She had been so confused about everything but now all that mattered was getting back to sailing. The mystery about this feeling business was intriguing but mostly annoying. She was so accustomed to having a soldier-up mentality Endure what you must and simply get to work. Feelings were not something anyone ever explained to Grayce. Stuff your emotions down deep where they belong. With an arrogant huff, she thought; "What good are feelings anyway? I have eyes."

She immediately felt remorse for that statement and sensed her attitude had transcended cocky. Grayce explained, "Luca, I wish I knew the fine line between knowing it all and thinking you know it all. I get mad, I rage, I break things. Then I get calm and everything tries to restore itself. It is becoming obvious to me I am missing out on something. What is it, Luca? Please help me learn?" Grayce was embarrassed again but decided a little soul baring to an angel was not wimpy; it was just smart.

"All my life I was taught to be in control of my own life, never depend on anyone or anything. Sheer will has directed everything I have done and it hurts that way. I am tired of being alone, Luca. I am over feeling like every decision is monumental. I want to stop agonizing over every mistake I have ever made. I want to forgive myself but do not know how." She began to cry. "Grayce you are all right. You are growing up and it does hurt at times. Everyone experiences pain, Grayce it is normal. There is a much better way. Trust me. You are ready to know about the calm. It is a gift we all give ourselves as we finally learn to trust in our Creator."

"Grayce, the calm is simply a decision to have unwavering trust in a higher intelligence. This force is always self correcting and runs the entire Universe. It corrects trillions of mistakes every second! It also gifts trillions of miracles every second! Can you imagine? It's almost impossible to fathom unless you believe. When you choose faith it all seems possible and the miracles start replacing mistakes. Life simply improves on all levels. To end the competition in your mind the battle of the ego must be fought. When you release being in control the calm comes over you like the sun warming the day after a raging storm passes."

"How do I find this calm Luca?" He smiled, "It is already here Grayce, just ask for it. Ask and it is given, the Kingdom of Heaven is within. It is called pure, holy love. Seek peace within yourself, Grayce and you will find it. Please just trust me Grayce, I know." No more words seemed important. They just all enjoyed the silence brought in by the presence of the eye of creation. Ranger was snoring and evidently missed it all. Animals so much smarter than we are, easing in and out of this calm like the wind. Brilliant she thought to herself, it is all beginning to make a little sense.

## Chapter Thirteen

# THE EYE

Luca began to explain innocence to Grayce. She noticed once again, it was still 4:02 am and raining. Time was becoming totally irrelevant. She busied herself with preparing the boat to sail. "Grayce I picked this child body to do your angel work because I had fun being a boy. I like being happy. Sadly, some people do not. Another person might relate to an older version of me, that happens. You can easily relate to my youthful self. My personal choice is innocence every time but even angels know about free will. Some people are quite stubborn and after they have forgotten their innocence, then they become quite hard to reach. We mostly begin to experience negative ideas or emotions as adults."

Luca lovingly rambled on. "We are free as children. We dream. We create. We have endless joy! Then we simply forget. We loose our innocence; then fear and doubt arrive. We start to believe people who tell us we should not dream so big. We are told we cannot try this or attempt that. It is impossible they might say. Without faith, we lose power in chasing our biggest desires. Sadly, we actually start to believe we are inadequate or unable to succeed with our dreams." That is just silly, Grace thought. "My dream is to sail around the globe. If you are coming along, why not help me with these ropes little boy?" She innocently wondered what the consequence of sassing an angel might be.

Suddenly, a warm breeze caused the main sail on *Silent Partner* to start flapping. The jib sail was not yet hoisted. It sat in a pile on the deck. Luca already knew what was coming next and had conveniently disappeared. Grayce had gone below to check the weather. She somehow missed a large storm system that had now fully encompassed Great Abaco and the other surrounding islands, too. In all her drama with Josh, she had also lost track of time. She was now yelling at herself and her heart raced. Ranger was miraculously still asleep on the front of the boat.

Frustration now fully set in, and her anger began to boil once more. She could not find anything she was looking for and was furious Luca had just simply gone away. The rage that fueled her earlier resumed savaging her thoughts and she was now crazed about the photo of Angus. How had her father known Mrs. Heartworth? When the large bolt of lightning struck the mast of the *Silent Partner* it caused a sudden shift in the boat, throwing both Grayce and Ranger overboard.

The wind gusts were picking up fast as the jib sail blew into the water. Ranger was frantically swimming around helplessly in a circle when Grayce was struck by the falling mast. She was knocked out instantly. Ranger was seriously entangled in the sinking jib sail as the thunder loudly roared in the massive storm above. Silence and peace is always there waiting below the surface of the water. Pain? Panic? Trust? There is a strange nothingness that overcomes a being when death approaches. A strange detachment occurs. A void opens a space without time. One beyond time feels only pure love. It is alluring and perfect. Everyone is given free will. Give up? Give in? Surrender? Choice is infinite. Who waits around for that? Grayce willed herself out of the water somehow. Or did she? What happens in the Eye cannot ever be fully explained.

## Chapter Fourteen

# POWER OF THE SUN

*Morning comes, it always does. The sun awakened the day as life resumed to normal after the wicked storm. Grayce resumed consciousness only to realize she was laying on the sandy beach, soaking wet. She had no idea what time it was or where Ranger was. She was afraid to open her eyes. The sun was warming her skin so she assumed it was day. Then she became aware her eyes were already open, however, they were not working. Odd she thought, eyes just do not decide to quit seeing. A large flock of pink flamingos flew overhead casting magical shadows over her small body. She heard the great birds but could not see them.*

*What is happening, I feel alive but I might be dead? Are my eyes now blind or am I paralyzed by fear? Dear God, she realized there was no more sight with this pair of eyes. They were finished. She only saw black, absolute darkness. Where did the sun go she thought? And, why am I here? Where is Ranger? Is he with God? Is he safe? But wait, the sun is still here. I can feel the warmth, that is real. What is real? Warmth is real, concentrate on the sun, period. The sand was warm too. If she trusted what she knew about sand and sun, then presumably she was safe. She lay back and sleep came again.*

The horrific reality Grayce must now face is that she survived a rogue wave experience as a result of the violent storm. It partially destroyed her sailboat and also temporarily blinded her. Ranger was one of many senseless victims of the fatal and tragic storm. No way he was able to navigate the punishing entanglement with the sinking jib sail. Grayce blamed herself relentlessly and relived the horror of Ranger's drowning at least one hundred times, probably more. He was a symbol now, a new reason for why she was doing this sail. Ranger's memory would have to be her rock now. His drowning image in her mind would fuel both, her rage and passion. Could tears fill an ocean? Grayce cried enough tears to fill ten oceans in that single moment. Will anything I love ever stay here with me or does death steal it all away, every single time?

Luca suddenly appeared, relaxed and happy like nothing had happened. *"Grayce, get up. We have sailing to do. Sight is only a matter of perception. I can be your eyes. If you have enough faith to overcome your temporary weakness and guilt we can do this together. I promise. Ranger is still a part of you and he always will be with you. Death is just a door for the soul to expand beyond the body. It is the same for Ranger. He is at peace. He is being loved by all that created us and that love never ends, ever. It is infinite and pure. Ranger found the Kingdom of Heaven, know that."* Grayce sadly moaned, "Luca I cannot go on this is pointless now. I cannot sail blind." She continued to cry buckets of tears. "Truthfully, I have no more faith Luca." And with that Luca was gone.

As soon as she realized Luca was gone, Grayce started hearing things differently. The world was strangely quiet and loud at the same time. The storm system was still hanging around. The luminous clouds started forming once again into thunderheads. Soon thereafter, loud claps of thunder began waking up this day. She heard the storm, instead of seeing it. The sun went away and the sky somehow now felt cold. She felt the sun go away and now knew her biggest asset was her ability to hear and feel. She might not see but she sure could still use her other senses.

She wondered what time it was and realized her watch was not only gone but now worthless. "I wonder if they make watches for the blind? Will I have to learn to read braille? How can I sail blind?" And with that she let out a horrific and very angry scream so loud it was probably heard on another island. It actually knocked the wind out of her and she fell onto the sand in a heap. Motionless, she thought if I lay still enough maybe it will be a dream. When I wake up, I will see. Grayce drifted away into a deep sleep.

*In her sleeping state, Grayce began to dream about the horses she had met the day before with Josh. The horse was an image she had always cherished. Sleep would now calm down her overactive mind. The dream continued. A majestic horse appeared with great wings, surrounded by the power of the sun. The horse was a dapple gray. It had a long, flowing white mane and tail. It was truly angelic in overall appearance. Pegasus? "Yes, Grayce, I am Pegasus."*

*"Your mother Frances sent me and Angus made the double ask, which created the miracle. Based upon both their desires for you, here I all in all my glory. I freely offer you infinite love and guidance. Rest. Sleep. Be at peace. Always know the creator loves you infinitely. Feel this all-powerful love every time you look at the sun. Remember Grayce you are and always will be a divine child of God."*

## Chapter Fifteen

# JOSH'S GIFT

*Dreams fill our minds with messages from our soul. Listen for the intention behind the dream for you are the one sending the message young one. Before sleep always remember to praise yourself and your loving Creator. In sleeping you fill your soul with energy for tomorrow. What fuel are you pouring in for your journey ahead? Can you allow others to give you love Grayce? Soften, bend, release, allow, trust in it all. You are infinitely loved.*

When Grayce woke up she recalled seeing a beautiful dapple gray horse with a young boy sitting on his back. She squinted her eyes and tried to make them work, but apparently they were still broken. Grayce thought she even smelled a horse so decided she probably lost her mind with her eyesight. Just then she definitely heard a familiar *whinny* sound knew there was a horse nearby. The smell was certain, too. Nothing replaces the divine smell of a horse. Confusion was starting to anger her when she heard a familiar voice. It was Josh. "Hello Grayce. Are you all right? We have all been so worried about you."

Josh was just now realizing that Grayce could not see and dismounted off his young, gray horse. He walked up and grabbed her small hand, "You are safe now, Grayce. Trust me everything is going to be just fine. Promise." She started to sob again, and strangely found herself without words. Her brain still worked, however, she was exceptionally happy Josh was here now. They just sat for a while until her heartbeat calmed down and her breathing had resumed to normal. Grayce broke the silence first, "I cannot see anything. I do not know where Ranger is. I am afraid he drowned. I am unsure what exactly happened to my boat. I am scared and all alone." Josh replied "Just try and relax Grayce. It will be all right."

"I am so mad at you Josh. Why are there photos of my father in your mother's guest cottage? I broke a frame and made a mess. I left without saying anything to your Mom and now I am angry and confused. Why did you not say anything?" Josh began to cry and said, "I am your half brother, Grayce. Mom and I figured it out after you left. She admitted to having an affair with Angus. It's complicated but she loves you. Don't feel bad about it. Is it an insane stroke of luck or is it destiny? Am I here to help now? Is that random or orchestrated? Grayce, we may never know all the answers to why. We do know now that we absolutely have each other. You have a family again! How awesome is that? It rocks. I seriously want to help you. Maybe you can help me and the horses, by continuing to spread the message about them?" Grayce whispered, "Yes, Josh my new half brother, thank you."

More help arrived, including Mrs. Heartworth who had been summoned. The locals rallied to get Grayce safely to the ER. It was ultimately determined she would be fine. A few day's rest was required before her sight would return to normal. Mrs. Heartworth insisted Grayce stay in the guest cottage and promised any unwanted photos would be put away. The local marina had all agreed to help restore the *Silent Partner* as best as they could. A new jib sail was ordered. Josh promised to stay by her side, until she was ready to sail. Even Amanda rallied, offering to put together a touching memorial service for Ranger. Love restores many things.

Josh came up with a fun way to show Grayce how much they all cared for her. It was going to be a global campaign designed to spread the idea to **Think Love.** Josh was having a huge load of these bracelets made up. The design was simple and made locally. It was constructed of natural hemp with a small heart charm attached that read, **Think Love.** The plan was to mail them to Grayce's destinations ahead of time.

*the Eye*

Josh figured it would help her make authentic, global connections with others based in love.

Josh was personally moved by a special organization he discovered online. It was located in Africa and called *"The Secret Love Project."* Josh knew social media could be dumb but also powerful when used in the right way. In Africa, the artist Michael Ellion is creating a community of love where countless, random hearts lead the way. Their primary aim is to spread love throughout the world. They are succeeding in creating global change. Josh was drawn to this organization out of appreciation and respect. He did not know anyone in Africa, but that did not matter. The message of love got through anyway.

In trying to help the wild Spanish Barb horses on Great Abaco Josh had unknowingly become something of a young philanthropist without any money. It is actually a powerful position to be in as it forces one to think out of the box and that is an attribute Josh certainly possessed. The secret weapon he creatively engaged for Grayce was Jimmy Buffet. Smart boy because Mr. Buffet unselfishly financed the whole **Think Love** bracelet campaign. Mr. Buffet even invited Mrs. Heartworth and Josh to attend his concert in Saint Lucia. Josh could not wait to tell Grayce; but remarkably restrained himself, for now.

Days came and went. Sleep is restorative. Home cooking is healing. A home built with love gives hope. Grayce slowly regained her strength and determination. Her sight was still quite blurry and no one agreed she was ready to sail on. Although, once her mind was made up there would be no stopping her. Josh devised another plan to protect Grayce until her sight was fully restored. "I can sail with you to Saint Lucia, Grayce. Just think about it because you will realize it could be fun. Without Ranger it will be tremendously sad and lonely out there. I can be your eyes for a couple of weeks, watch over you and make you laugh. I know you will go stubbornly on without me when you are ready." Grayce stunned him when without hesitation, she just smiled and said, "deal." **In that single moment true grace awakened in her.**

## Chapter Sixteen

# SAINT LUCIA

*The higher level of thought continued to stream through her mind. Grayce hated to admit it and would not say this out loud yet, it was fun sailing with Josh. It somehow softened her. The air smelled better, the wind cooperated and it was nice being together. I am grateful for Josh, thank you Angus. I forgive you, Angus. And with that she let go of all the anger she had towards her father and took a deep breath in. Breathing out she wished him peace. She also prayed for the ability to remember this the first time she got irritated or frustrated with Josh. Angel work sure is exhausting it easier to stay mad. Silently, she affirmed I will try.*

Sailing away from Great Abaco without Ranger would have seemed impossible had it not been for Josh. His agreeing to travel along with Grayce to Saint Lucia was just the thing to put her attitude back together. Grayce was an expert sailor and everyone around her knew this fact. Sadly, her normal confidence was quite rattled. The challenge of losing Ranger and her sight, even if only for a few days, was punishing. Now she needed to show the world she could sail again. Josh provided a secret distraction from her shock and sadness which proved quite healing. They had smooth sailing for a while so small talk was fun. Now the fact that they were half siblings was present, conversation was somehow easier.

"You know Josh I have never really had anyone to really talk to about anything besides Ranger. You are the first person I have told many private things to; it is nice to share. It is scary to have faith in someone. I didn't know that I could trust you until the storm. The way you came to my side and gave up everything for me is absolutely the bomb. Bless you brother." As most males do when topics get even slightly mushy, Josh went silent. Finally, he said something. "I figured you would be mad at me forever. Holy cow, I am so relieved you aren't anymore, that is scary!" They both cracked up thinking about this unexpected, divine connection. Then decided it was time for some coconut juice and pineapple.

Sailing was great, so was the snack. They didn't need to talk for now. Josh was really excited about returning to Saint Lucia. It had been years since he had spent any time there. Located in the eastern Caribbean Sea between Saint Vincent, Barbados, and Martinique, it's wildly popular with sailors. Such a beautiful destination he thought. Wow, Grayce was so smart to have plotted her next stop there. He filled time with a story about the actor Matt Damon, whom he loved. Matt had rented out an entire resort on Saint Lucia in 2013 to renew his wedding vows to Luciana Barbroso.

Saint Lucia was also world famous for the black sand beach called *Anse Mamin*, where he secretly hoped they could moor her boat nearby and snorkel. The pristine beaches are all perfectly adorned with thriving coconut trees, tiki huts, and hammocks. It's a favorite global destination for happy people lucky enough to go there. It was right then, in the middle of a normal conversation, the love book fell onto the floor of the boat. Grayce laughed. She had seen this before. "Josh, the book has something to teach us." Josh had nothing to say to that, but still managed to smiled. The book of love had fallen open to a new page. Grayce it read to him.

### Knowledge and Half-Knowledge

*"Four frogs sat upon a log that lay floating on the edge of a river. Suddenly the log was caught by the current and*

swept slowly down the stream. The frogs were delighted and absorbed, for never before had they sailed.

At length the first frog spoke, and said, 'this is indeed a most marvelous log. It moves as if alive. No such log was ever known before.'

Then the second frog spoke and said, 'Nay my friend, the log is like other logs, and does not move. It is the river that is walking to the sea, and carries us and the log with it.'

And, the third frog spoke and said; 'It is neither the log nor the river that moves. The moving is in our thinking. For without thought nothing moves.'

And then three frogs began to really wrangle about what was moving. The quarrel grew hotter and hotter but they could not agree. They then turned to the fourth frog, who up to this time had been listening attentively but holding his peace, and they asked his opinion.

And, the fourth frog said, 'Each one of you is right and none of you is wrong. The moving is in the log and in the water and our thinking also.'

And the three frogs became very angry, for none of them was willing to admit, that his was not the whole truth, and that the other two were not wholly wrong.

Then the strange thing happened. The three frogs got together and pushed the fourth frog off the log and into the river." *Kahlil Gibran*

They just looked at each other and grinned. Grayce finally broke the silence. "What do you think it means, Josh?" He laughed and loved knowing she actually cared about his thoughts. "It is an incredible poem and a valuable lesson, I think. He is teaching us that together we can achieve great things. When we isolate and mistrust others get snuffed out. Then we learn nothing new and achieve even less." Grayce was impressed. Josh truly had a deep respect for nature, learning new things, and the islands. This was clear. And, he knew quite a lot for his age. The result of plenty of self imposed studying. Josh enjoyed sharing what he knew with Grayce. It seemed to both compliment and soften her maritime expertise. She lightened it up a bit, "Well I promise not to act like a frog and push you off the boat!" They giggled again and it was good.

Josh further explained; "The Saint Lucia beaches are protected by local a marine sanctuary. The result is an extremely healthy ecosystem of coral and reef fish. I wish we had one around Great Abaco. It would help a lot of problem areas to be restored. Saint Lucia's local fishing communities are healthy and prosperous too. It's a win-win for all." Josh had been there as a child when his mom took him there once on a spontaneous trip. He assumed Angus had introduced his mom to the island. He decided leaving that part out for now was wise. Grayce was definitely not ready for the intensity of another Angus conversation. Josh guessed anger was probably still under the surface. He definitely respected that.

Josh then told her about the bracelets. Grayce was beyond excited about the **Think Love** idea. And, they would be attending the Jimmy Buffet concert. The crowd there would receive the first batch of free gifts. Grayce had a big grin on her face. Josh added, "Saint Lucia is a popular concert venue for Mr. Buffet. He loves the Beause'jour Stadium. The stadium is world famous for awesome matches of cricket. The stadium holds 20,000 fans and has lighting at night. It was the first stadium in the Caribbean to have floodlights installed in 2006. Mr. Buffet has held an annual concert there ever since. The locals who cherish his music fill the stadium year after year. How cool is that?"

Josh's curiosity ignited now, "Grayce, how does it feel to know you are starting a peaceful, global movement with the bracelet?" She hesitated before answering in hopes of sounding intelligent. She amazed herself as these words seemed to flow out of nowhere; ***"Grace is gifted to us all when we forgive and return to thinking about love."*** Josh sighed and replied, "Well you go girl, looks like a sage is born!" They both laughed out loud. For the first time Grayce was actually starting to believe it. She decided to keep that part to herself for now.

Time marches on. The concert exceeded expectations on all levels. There is channel of love that exists between strangers when accessed.

Concerts, cricket and even horse shows may create unity. A happy venue is anywhere people are all enjoying the same experience. They are here now. Not somewhere else. The *Think Love* bracelets were now everywhere. Filling up the night with thoughts of love, long after the music had stopped playing. Jimmy Buffet had really put on a fabulous show. A feeling of joy and bliss permeated the air. Grayce was singing her favorite sailor lines all the way back to her boat.

> **"Nautical Wheelers who call them selves sailors, play fiddle under the stars.**
>
> **It's dance with me, dance with me, Nautical Wheelers, take me to stars that you know."**
>
> **Jimmy Buffet**

Grayce was now ready to move on alone. It was time. Her independence was back in full force. Josh and Grayce shared a long good bye hug and tears did flow. As Josh watched her sail off he counted his many blessings. More tears rolled down his cheeks. He asked Grayce's angels to watch over his beautiful new sister on her fantastic journey. The *Silent Partner* eventually crossed over the horizon and its lights disappeared from sight. "Bye little sis. Sweet sailing. Please be safe and strong. I know you will always find the best winds." Josh almost passed out when three whales breached nearby. He quickly decided his prayer's had just been answered and closed his eyes.

## Chapter Seventeen

# LADY PALM

*Grayce's higher level thoughts gently rolled around like calm ocean waves. Solitude is a funny thing; it allows you to become fully exposed to all things divine. And then at some point you wake up and there is an invisible force driving the boat. I suppose it is energy, like the wind. Migration patterns of animals, marine mammals and birds present this perfect energy to us with nature's choreography and ballet. Practice God's will in all you do until it is you. Island hopping around the coast off Brazil provided the symphony of nature Grayce always loved. The gently swaying palm trees attracted incredible giant Blue McCaw parrots like bees to honey. Grayce noticed they were always in pairs. I guess they need each other too. She enjoyed that thought and smiled.*

Grayce was becoming more used to these new, random streams of thought, even amused. Navigating the small islands and coves in between vast stretches of open sea, she came across a floating box of oranges. Impulsively, she almost dove in! Instinctively, she denied the urge and looked for the reaching pole instead. After finding the useful pole, she watched the box for a while. It was amusing to imagine where the box had been. "Where would it eventually go? Who would find it and on what beach? And, where was Luca? I miss that stupid boy. If I need the oranges and will use them, perhaps they were meant for me. Is this a miracle or simply luck? Maybe I will plant a few seeds and prove you can grow an orange tree while sailing the globe solo. Yes, I like it, why not? Is that greedy? Maybe I should share them with others at my next stop."

She had enough of this silly debate and reached out with the pole. The claw hook on the end was perfectly designed to do the grabbing work. It was actually an antique that had belonged to Winston. She missed a few times and almost fell overboard. Watching a few black tip reef sharks swimming near the box she was most grateful for her boat. Finally, persistence paid off resulting in fresh squeezed orange juice. Grayce savored the sweet juice and stored the box down below.

**As she remembered to thank Winston for the pole in that moment, the Creator knowingly put forth another series of miracles for her. Heaven arrives in the middle of the ocean in the most unexpected of ways.**

Grayce had a new confidence sailing into Rio De Janeiro; but she had no idea what a local fortune teller, would soon reveal to her. Understanding anger can reveal larger powers at work. She had a multitude of things to consider doing in Brazil. She thought about how the world is simply an ever expanding universe. What should I do first? Perhaps a new tattoo? Music and dance celebration? Tarot reading? Astrology? Numerology? Yes, she absolutely was looking forward to all Brazil had to offer. When she sailed by the world famous, *"Christ the Redeemer"* art deco statue, she contemplated finding a church to attend. She then changed her mind remembering she didn't even go to church.

The marina in Rio De Janeiro was much larger than any she had sailed into before. She was astonished by the assortment of sailboats, all sizes and all colors. There were a lot of small wooden boats. The boats were painted with bright colors of red, green or blue. They were very different from Key West. The old boats have great character. They tell a story, similar to scars on people. Key West boats are mostly fiberglass and white, not many scars. Family life was everywhere in the marina, more so than in Florida. She noticed many kids with their mothers and grandmothers playing on some of boats. It was early afternoon. She decided it must be the siesta time after lunch.

After securing the *Silent Partner* in a slip, it was time for a visit to town for supplies. Locating the marina office and manager proved easy enough. Grayce paid for the boat space and thanked the manager. On the way out of the office she stopped. On the wall there was a paper flyer tacked to a cork board with other business cards. It caught her eye because of the beautiful artwork.

***Lady Palm. Discover a deck of ancient Polynesian tarot cards. Always enlightened and generous to any person who is willing. The defenseless person armed with nothing but love invites miracles into life. The person who listens becomes a person of inspired action and infinite peace.***

Grayce just had to have it, "May I please take this flyer?" The manager grinned like a young boy. "Sure, take any thing on that board you like; that's why it's there." Grayce gently untacked the flyer, folded it up and jammed it in her backpack. "Thank you again. See you later."

Grayce called for an Uber taxi and sat down to consider the information on the flyer. How absolutely amazing this Lady Palm must be! I wonder if she will have time for a reading with me? Uber arrived shortly thereafter and knew where the Lady Palm lived. After driving past the world's most famous beach, the *Copacabana*, Grayce was not particularly impressed. That must be the most human beings ever in one place, she thought. Cracking up, she realized they looked like a mass of beached Elephant seals. The people were everywhere! Give me sailing solo over tourism any day, affirming her unwavering independence.

It wasn't long and they arrived at Lady Palm's residence. Grayce paid the driver and thanked her. The driver surprised Grayce by replying, "Have fun, Grayce, she is a real game changer. Do listen to her; it's worth it. All locals know she is deeply connected to everything ethereal. Lady Palm is extremely intelligent." Grayce grinned and got out of the car. She already loved the place. The front door was painted blue along with all the windows. Flowers and palm trees beautified the house and yard. It was different from Mrs. Heartworth's cottage; but definitely had the same loving, inviting aura surrounding it.

Grayce walked up to the blue door and knocked. A stunning woman answered and introduced herself. "Hello, I am the Lady Palm, welcome." Grayce saw a beautiful multi colored scarf tied around her head like a turban. She also noticed Lady Palm wore a long, flowing white linen dress. Lady Palm was barefoot. Grayce was barefoot, too. Instantly enchanted, Grayce was totally without words. "Come in young one. Follow me this way to my table of harmony and cards." There were cut flowers everywhere in hand painted vases. The ceiling was incredible, a high arched roof with exposed wood beams. Small crystal chimes were hung from the beams. The skylight above let the sun light in, casting an enchanting prism on the wall.

"By the way, what is your name sweet one? And, do you know why you are here?" Lady Palm was really beautiful and obviously gentle. "Yes, my name is Grayce. I would really like a tarot card reading with you." Lady Palm graciously held out her hand leading her up a flight of stairs. She then showed Grayce into her scared reading room. It was everything Grayce expected; candles, incense, tarot cards, crystal charms and carved wooden statues. It was all so terribly intriguing. No photos anywhere; very interesting Grayce thought. Lady Palm asked Grayce to sit down and said, "You are a lucky young woman. Divine powers perfectly at work today. I just had a last minute cancellation. You may certainly now have the time slot."

"What is your full name, Grayce?" She replied, "Grayce Kelly Kingston." Very blessed girl, Lady Palm thought. "Grayce fortunately you have two letter K's in your name which is one of the luckiest gifts you could ever receive. It means you are an open channel for higher energy. The letter K is open on the top and the bottom, you see. That means you are a receptor for higher, light energy from our Creator above. And, you are available for the grounding, loving energy from Mother Earth below. This is a sacred blessing and must be appreciated. Very cool young one."

Lady Palm lit some sweet smelling incense. "Are you comfortable now, Grayce?" Secretly, Grayce was totally afraid but did not want fear that to show. There was regret in her over the negative way she had treated people in the past. There was deep shame for the angry thoughts that insistently ruled her mind. "Yes, Lady Palm, I am. Thank you." A respectful pause filled the room. Lady Palm turned over the Polynesian Tarot cards on the table. The images were spectacular; based upon marine mammals, sea creatures and birds. Dolphin, Whale, Albatross, Moray Eel, White Pelican, Sea Lion, Sea Turtle where among the ones Grayce noticed. The rest of the world seemed to go away and an aura of peace came over them both.

Lady Palm asked Grayce to shuffle the cards and cut them. Grayce complied, shuffling the artistic cards and nervously making a cut. Grayce then politely placed her hands in her lap. She wondered if Lady Palm could sense how was nervous. "Now, Grayce I will hold them and you pick seven cards." After the selection, Lady Palm spread the cards around the table.

*"All right Grayce, just relax and listen. The first card drawn is the great Albatross. This is your true ally and ultimate protector. The Albatross card in this position means you are on a great adventure, a solo journey."*

Grayce almost laughed out loud but did manage to only smile. "I see that pleases you, Grayce. do Feel absolutely free to share any thoughts that come up. It is all good sweet one." Grayce all but squealed, "I am currently sailing around the world alone!" They both just looked at each other for a brief moment, then simply burst out laughing. A joyous, tangible energy filled the room. There was now an invisible balance between the fully bonded souls.

Lady Palm regained her elegant tranquility by refocusing her intent. "Clearly, I am gifted at what I do. This, however, is beyond me young one. This is undoubtedly divine. It's a beautiful thing. Let's proceed and have some fun. Shall we Grayce?" Lady Palm flashed a huge smile. Grayce responded, "Yes please Lady Palm." It got quiet again, Grayce watched the card reader go fully inside herself. She breathed deeply and a notable stillness permeated the room. It was pretty cool; Grayce hated to admit. This spiritual stuff really confuses me, she thought. Too bad Luca isn't here. He would tell me if this is for real or not.

> *"Grayce calm your thoughts. It is time to be at peace. Release your fear based thoughts. Replace them with gratitude. Under your intense fears lie sleeping joy. This is your eternal birthright but you must claim it for yourself. Your Albatross card carries the following unique message for you."*

> *"Love holds to Earth. Earth holds to Sun. Sun holds to Galaxy. Galaxy is Infinite. Infinite is Peace. Peace is Love. Love is Freedom. Freedom is Flight. Soar with the strength of the Albatross who flies alone for months out at sea. He is always guided by everything Divine. His strength is yours now So it is. So be it. Amen."*

Lady Palm slowly read every card revealing many higher consciousness thoughts to Grayce. Like a mother, she expressed many new ways for Grayce to perceive the world based experience. They talked about family and love. They shared about pain and loss. They debated about resentments and anger. Lady Palm explained about subtle power, how masculine and feminine energies will enhance your life by using both. They contemplated new hopes and lost dreams. Lady Palm does not ever discuss fear. Lady Palm then calmly began channeling something much higher again.

> *"Grayce I see that you have simply forgotten what harmony really means. You believe because your Earth family is gone, you are alone or separate. That is just not true. Your family has not gone anywhere they are now everywhere, instead. Your anger has served you well, sweet one. The rage fueled you to find a better way. This led you to me now. Surrender and appreciate all painful experiences. This is the only way to honestly grow and grow you must. The body will*

*eventually die. You must begin to ask what will your spirit have learned here?"*

*"Spirit cannot die for it is infinite. That is law based truth. Embrace a new way of thinking. Then watch yourself create the village or new family needed to complete your life. This process of change for you, Grayce, must be based on love never regret. Sail in faith not fear. Remember this always. Discovering your unique spirit is the pinnacle of all life, Grayce. Not your everyday human goals. As you tap into your higher self these divine aspirations begin to attain themselves. Always directed by the self organizing Creator of the universe. He loves you unconditionally. You will reach great achievement as you learn to allow, not control."*

Lady Palm then wrote something down for Grayce and handed her the paper with these words, **Happiness is Peace. Peace is Love. Love is Happiness.** "This is a divine mantra Grayce. It is now uniquely yours to keep. Treasure the words and allow them to guide you when you feel lost. Also, Grayce, I will ask you to keep this very special deck of Polynesian tarot cards. I do not normally give anything away but I know you will be guided by them on your voyage. It makes me happy to know they can help you on your sail. Use them with your internal quest, too. With gratitude and love I extend you happiness, peace and joy, always!"

Grayce internalized the loving sentiment while feeling a supreme state of tranquility. Suddenly, the doorbell rang right when an egg timer went off. Grayce didn't want to leave but knew it was time. "That is my next client. We must now say good bye but we will never be apart. Know that in your precious heart, Grayce. Be the joy and seek peace." Grayce gave Lady Palm a big hug and tears flowed. Grayce whispered, "Oh my, thank you for the cards. The reading was truly more than I expected. The cards will be appreciated when my heart has big questions. I promise to use them often. And, I will try to trust my higher self more. Wow. Bless you."

After the illuminating tarot session with Lady Palm Grayce felt great. She already had her new mantra memorized. She had new understanding that her feelings were a choice, that sure felt refreshing. Chose love not anger. Choose forgiveness not judgment. Choose happiness not tears. Choose acceptance not resistance. So many new things to remember. Another wonderful woman showing Grayce how to live an exceptionally authentic life was unforgettable. Now thinking she might grow into a lady someday seemed much less scary. Grayce was pleased to have enjoyed Brazil in such an enlightening way. She was not interested anymore in the other ways to spend time in Brazil. Grayce decided nothing else mattered except getting back to her quest. Now, she was ready to sail on to Africa.

Grayce put the tarot cards in her backpack and called again for Uber. The mind habitually started churning out relentless thoughts again. She realized they were not all negative. "Time to go get the *Silent Partner* ready to sail once more. This is my life. Today, I can honestly see how proud I am of myself. I wonder how long before I forget all I learned here today? How will I remember all of these expansive ideas? Do I deserve such happiness? And, where is Luca? Holy cow Grayce, you are now talking out loud to yourself. What's next? Someone else sailing the boat for you?" She simply grinned.

## Chapter Eighteen

# WHITE PELICANS

Grayce was elated knowing the sail across to Africa would be sprinkled with abundant marine life and more unique migration patterns. It was not long before the waves began to put Grayce in her beloved space of peace. She was more easily finding harmony in her thoughts. Sailing was truly the one place she was free. It reminded her of a favorite quote by Albert Einstein; *"I like sailing because it is the sport which demands the least energy."* Einstein is so right, she thought. Sailing is almost effortless at times. Spinner dolphins appeared as if on cue. They effortlessly and systematically swam along side the boat. Grayce knew it was all choreographed by the Creator himself. Home again. The ocean really is where I belong. She bowed her head in thanks.

Her inner voice calmly whispered; *Feel the intensity of the sun. It heightens the connection to the Creator. How blessed you are to live on Earth? Contemplate the sun. It warms you. It wakes up the entire world without asking, day after, day after, day. The sun does not choose to shine on just a few, instead it always shines freely on you all.*

*That is what pure love is all about. It is not selective, rather it includes all. Think about how everyone stares at the sunset. It's a universal act all people share across the globe. Why? You all collectively feel the Creator's love. You are all equally at home in the warmth of the sun. God speaks to you all through the sun. Watch for the white pelicans they are coming to you soon.*

Grayce was becoming more familiar with the higher consciousness voice in her head. What a concept this is, turn off the mind noise and let the divine music play. It is simply brilliant, she laughed at herself. I have got to remember the astonishing truth, about universal acceptance. She giggled, wildly amused by her new ability to have dialog with herself. As badly as she missed Ranger, she now fully realized she might not ever be lonely again. It was clear Grayce was beginning to more fully trust herself.

White pelicans this far out to sea, no way! This higher intelligence business was pretty cool but she did not fully trust it quite yet. Grayce could drop into her stream of believing in angels, faith and trust. She could also still get mad and quickly fall out of the stream. Seems one moment I believe and then I am not sure. For so long, I have been claiming seeing angels my truth. Only now though, do I begin to understand what it means. Nothing good happens when you are angry all the time. The angels only exist when my heart is open, calm and loving. Perhaps I am growing up? Just then, Grayce had a thought, maybe it is time to get another dog. When I find him I will name him *Einstein* and a huge smile adorned her tan, youthful face.

Several days into this stretch of smooth sailing, a large flock of white pelicans actually appeared. For a moment Grayce was simply lost in the beauty of their flight. Then she wondered why they were so far out to sea. Pelicans always reminded Grayce of Winston. She longed for her Grandfather badly but still remained angry at his senseless death. Men; they are absolutely pathetic in so many areas of life. She recalled a very funny story about Winston and Angus that helped shape her independence. Winston had a huge Blue Samsonite suitcase on his houseboat that belonged to Frances. As a little girl, Grayce loved playing with the giant bag. Always imagining what her mother might have put in it. It was so spacious she could actually curl up in it.

One blistering hot Key West afternoon, Grayce had made another mess cooking for Angus and Winston. Something irritated Winston which was sadly a frequent in their lives. He thoughtlessly yelled at

Grayce about the mess, so she determined to run away. Grayce stomped around the houseboat right past Angus and Winston. She ran down the narrow stairs into the galley kitchen. Winston and Angus were oddly amused. She was crying so hard she almost threw up. Grayce still managed to pull the suitcase out of the closet. She confidently put a tattered t-shirt and a polka dot swim suit in the big blue Samsonite. Trying to drag the huge bag up the tiny stairs was almost impossible. She stubbornly proceeded ahead with her plan. Making it upstairs, Grayce sat down in exhaustion. The bag looked enormous and she hoped they would not look inside.

Winston looked up over his reading glasses and calmly said, "Looks like you're going away, Grayce?" There was a long pause and an eerie silence. The tears were drying for the moment. Her breathing had returned somewhere near normal. "I am running away from home," she defiantly announced. Without hesitation, Winston fired back, "Honey, you are going to need some spending money." Reaching into his dirty Levi jean shirt pocket, he smiled. Pulling out a single one-dollar bill, Winston offered it to Grayce. She angrily snatched it right up without hesitation. She accidentally knocked over Winston's favorite concrete pelican statue with the suitcase on her way out.

***Unknowingly, the guilt of that innocent act would haunt and taint her future decisions in this life. Guilt causes separation. We all get lost until we remember to forgive ourselves and others for everything. Through forgiveness the guilt simply vanishes.***

Angus tried hard not to laugh, even though he knew there was cruelty behind the joke. Tears began to fill her eyes again as she opened the suitcase and placed the dollar bill softly on her tiny t-shirt. She closed the bag and dragged it off the boat and down the long dock. The boys just quietly watched her go away. Grayce decided to hide out in the marina dump. Smelly place to wait on any rescue plan. Extremely smelly! The dump at a marina has lots of dead fish parts. With those two man-children in charge of any rescue, Grayce might be waiting a very long time.

Obstinately, Grayce concluded it was worth any foul odor to punish them. So let the waiting began. Grayce actually waited all night. They never looked for her until late afternoon the next day. In the end, it turns out they knew where she had been hiding. So she was probably not in any danger hiding in the dump or so they thought. The defiant and angry side of Grayce certainly emerged that night. It was still randomly fueling her today. Mind games. We learn them early. It's incredible how such a small event can shape a mind. It was clear now it did help her gain a sense of independence early, which is exactly why she was on this trek. Grayce snickered at herself. "I love my suitcase story," she whispered. She gave thanks for this crazy thing called life.

Night rolled by again, there was a thick marine layer everywhere. When it was 4:02 am, a full moon suddenly lit up the sky. The white pelicans appeared again and were flying in unison with the boat. Just then Luca appeared. "Hi Grayce! I missed you." Grayce was so excited to see her little friend. "Oh Luca I am so happy you have returned, thank you. Where were you? I needed you!" He grinned and marveled at the independent little girl. ***You only need yourself Grayce. I am always here. When you remember to trust in this blessed law of the universe, we will never ever feel apart again.***

"Think about when you are sailing Grayce. It is something you are an expert at, there is no doubt. You fully trust yourself out anywhere on the open sea. There is no doubt because you are in your perfection on purpose. By the way, I loved your suitcase story too. That is why I am here again. You are starting to really connect with us, by loving yourself. The more you dial into that higher side of you, the easier we can communicate. It's always available but you absolutely have to remember to trust in it. Anger shuts it down completely, so does judgment and blame."

"Grayce, you have a special angel coming who has been wanting to visit you for a long while now. Your heart has been too closed off for him to reach you. I sense that is different now so I think you should expect to see your Grandfather, Winston soon. Be easy with him, Grayce. Revisiting your anger and old issues is useless, a total waste of your energy. Do not let your ego shove out love, do not let pride destroy joy. Independence is amazing, co-creation is even better. Sadly, when manifesting your dreams is done with anger using hateful memories that fuel, that is bad karma. Sorry, Grayce but you reap what you sew. And, honestly that is just bad mojo that never stops. Your ability to connect with Winston is based upon your own surrender and willingness. Are you ready to forgive him, Grayce?" Luca already knew the answer.

**They remained silent a while as the extraordinary white pelicans continued to fly along side the Silent Partner. Present was a calm sea, a full moon and a healing golden light beaming down into the vast depth of blue. There was also a breathing, living body of pure energy that the boat just kind of floated on. It exists outside of time; the calm, the Eye, the presence of all things divine. Yes, it was quite tangible. Like no decision could ever be needed there because no problems exist in the Eye. We are being taken care of by something much better at solving things than us. No questions asked. Just a little wind needed and a lot of gratitude. Miracles are real. Peace exists everywhere, all the time. Especially in the middle of the ocean at 4:02 am under a full moon.**

Very early the next morning Grayce spotted Africa. A surge of confidence over came her. Grayce actually did a little dance on the boat. This is huge, I made it! Luca had left again but this time she did not seem to mind. Two days sailing past the massive continent caused her to reflect on the countless, tragic problems the planet faces. She thought a lot about Nelson Mandela and his awe-inspiring accomplishments. There was an island just off Cape Town she was sailing towards called Robbin Island. It is where Nelson Mandela served out most of his cruel, inhumane punishment after being banished. She was overcome by a strange sadness. Grayce hated admitting the world can really be an evil place. Changing the stream of thoughts, she recalled Josh had already sent the **Think Love** bracelets here. Her arrival was anticipated by the local officials. It was a mixed bag of feelings to be sure. *Deciding not to give into her alter of anxiety,* Grayce sailed on.

Upon reaching Robbin Island she sailed into the marina. Confidently, Grayce wheeled the *Silent Partner* into a slip. As expected, the local officials were there. It was a warm welcome and Grayce was touched. Josh had also arranged for the artist Michael Ellion who started the *"The Secret Love Project,"* to meet Grayce there. Michael kindly agreed to help the distribute her bracelets to the locals. She was so grateful. He then told her about a huge statue he created. It is a giant pair of Ray Ban sunglasses. Michael explained how he appreciated that Nelson Mandela always wore Ray Bans. The unique artistic endeavor and national tribute is called, *"Perceiving Freedom."* People from all over the world visit the statue everyday of the year. This all delighted Grayce. Sincerely, she vowed to always stay in touch with her new African friends.

Later in the day and back on her boat, Grayce put some Jimmy Buffet on her I-Pad. She noticed it was exactly 4:02 p.m. She cracked up and shook her head. One of her favorite songs, *"African Friend"* was playing. Serendipitous? No, definitely angels she insisted to herself. Grayce could not stop smiling. Hoisting the sails, she was eager to start sailing around the rest of Africa. Grayce would travel to the paramount chain of islands called Seychelles. She felt calm. And, she felt protected. Exactly like when in the eye of a storm. Today, however, there was a clear, blue sky. There were no storms anywhere. Grayce finally believed in herself. Trusting in her dreams was making them all a reality. Perhaps she could find this unique calm on her own, after all. Sighing deeply, she gave thanks to her Creator, again and again and again. When the love book fell down in the galley, she could not wait to read what was on the page this time. It read;

*"God turns you from one feeling to another and teaches you the means of opposites, so that you will have two wings, not one.*

*Sadness is but a wall between two gardens.*

*Trust in dreams, for in them is hidden the gate to eternity."*
*Kahlil Gibran*

*Chapter Nineteen*

# WINSTON KINGSLEY

When Grayce saw Winston sitting on the boat she almost fell overboard. "Hello Grayce. It's alright, just relax. I have been watching you always, we have never been apart. I am so proud of you little girl. You are doing so well on your voyage. What a sailor you have become!" Grayce was speechless for only a brief moment. "What you are here, just like that? Have you been watching and waiting? Then do you steely determine when to appear? It seems mean." Grayce shocked even herself with her coldness. "No Granddaughter, I thought it was time I told you why Angus and I named the boat *Silent Partner*. You see I knew that we both would leave this world before you dear, Grayce. We wanted to leave a message to you that would always be a symbol of our love. You know Angus loved horses. We never told you about his first pony, who was named *Silent Partner*. At the time I bought the pony, they were both only seven years old."

Grayce calmed down and listened. "Angus loved that pony, I mean that is all he ever wanted to do. I tried to get him to follow me into the lucrative sport fishing business with me but he would have nothing to do with it. Stubborn boy. Everyday, all he looked forward to was riding that pony. Grayce, you know I was not a soft man. I always made Angus do a lot of hard chores on the docks and boats. The pony was a reward. We actually kept the little thing down at the old marina on Key West, in a little corral we built. Key West was really small then and everyone knew everything about everyone. The entire town loved this pony too. Angus even had his photo in the local paper when he rode that beloved pony of his in a Fourth of July parade."

"One hot summer a storm blew in and made a real mess of things. Some boats tipped over and some just sunk. We were all without electricity for many days. This punishing storm just dragged on and on. Angus worried about that pony but I kept telling him it would be all right. Well, actually it wasn't because the pony had been hit by lightning and died instantly. Right there in the corral at the marina. It was awful. We decided to never talk about that pony again, and we never did. I think that is one of the deep scars that kept Angus and myself locked in a silent misery. My drinking really took off after that very sad event. You obviously know the rest of my life story."

"Anyways, to his credit, Angus never gave up on his horse dreams. After high school he went off to Palm Beach to seek them out. Many years later, after we restored your boat, the idea came to me about the name. I asked Angus if he liked it and, of course, he did. So we named your boat *Silent Partner* in honor of that silly pony. We silently tried rather unsuccessfully forgive ourselves. Every day I secretly hoped that little pony found God. While living I did not have much faith, Grayce. Luckily God is infinitely forgiving and infinitely merciful. Granddaughter, now you know the reason behind the boat name. Every time you think about the name, *Silent Partner,* simply trust we are right here with you always. We love you, Grayce."

"Grandfather, I cannot believe it is you. I am so sorry for being mad at you for so long. It was so hard when you died. You were more of a father to me than Angus; we all know that. But when I found out you drank yourself to death I was furious! What a stupid thing to do, why Grandfather? You left me all alone, I had no one. Why?"

"Life is hard Grayce. I came from nothing and built something. I got very ego driven and destroyed many innocent people on my selfish way to the top. I made money and became greedy, very greedy. And, equally cruel and judgmental. I lost a lot along the way. Resentments and anger destroyed me. Death took away all those I loved except you.

Actually, Grayce in the real world sense, I lost it all except you. It is not an excuse but pain causes people to do really dumb things. Grayce, would you please forgive me?" Grayce did not hesitate; **"Of course Grandfather, of course I will. I do forgive you!"** And, with that simple act of forgiveness, a new series of miracles were instantly set into motion by the Creator.

Grayce was navigating a small series of islands and reefs so sailing was slow, cautious, inspiring, and precious. This was Seychelles, it was beyond beautiful. 116 islands make up the incredible chain. Seychelles is in the Indian Ocean and bordered by the Atlantic. Perfectly designed for sailing, Grayce loved it. She felt pride in knowing how far she had come on her journey. Grayce realized, this was another example of beauty and harmony existing in the middle of the ocean. Peace is where you find it. It happens. It exists. There is no chaos in a self correcting world.

*I must somehow let people know there is a great peace in simplicity and in the natural world. I made mistakes that I now always attempt to correct. Mistakes are now in the past. I do not reside in the past. The past is no where. I chose to be here now. I now, many more times create miracles that now positively change my world. A sage is indeed born. I will make a difference. Thank you my beloved Creator, for it all.*

Grayce enjoyed more incredibly relaxed conversation with Winston. Soon enough, they decided to anchor the boat for a stop. After they secured the *Silent Partner* in a quiet cove, Grace heard a little barking sound from the beach. She decided to go check it out. Winston followed her, too. Right there on the beach, in the shade under a palm tree, was a mother dog with her litter of puppies.

Winston told Grayce it was a gift from the Creator, she was free to choose a puppy. "There are huge rewards for walking in forgiveness, never forget that. Sadly, Grayce, I stupidly blocked out that part. I never taught you anything about it. You cannot teach what you do not know, period. Your ignorance should not to be judged. It just is. Grace is given when we forgive, again and again and again. **We are all God awakening**." A brave little male puppy made its way across the sand, right to where they stood. He wagged his tail wildly and just sat down right in front of Grayce. "Oh my, Grandfather just look at my adorable new puppy! I will call him Einstein." She picked him up and the tears began again. This time they were tears of joy, not sorrow.

Back on the boat and sailing once more, the air was carrying a scent of love. Winston shared many stories about Angus and Frances that Grayce had not heard before. These were the happy stories in the beginning and they were sweet. She was delighted in knowing they were once in love. Grayce now truly understood she was born out of this precious love. It softened the wounds and she realized Luca and Rumi were absolutely right. The light really does come in through the wounds. "Thank you Grandfather, I love you!"

Softly, Winston said, "I love you too dear, granddaughter. Sail on girl, you got this. I will always be with you." She closed her eyes. Seconds later, Grayce knew Winston was gone. Thank God, Einstein was still here, she thought. Einstein just sat there in adoration, joyously wagging his little puppy tail. The great white pelicans were now back flying alongside the *Silent Partner*. Grayce was really grateful for the magnificent bird's presence. There would be no more sadness today. She had found her garden outside of the wall and she liked it there. Her life garden was now being fertilized with pure grace. A gift from the Creator and she absolutely knew it. Grayce hugged little Einstein. Then she let the sweet tears of joy roll gently down her face, once more.

*Chapter Twenty*

# THINK LOVE

*Josh kept shipping the bracelets to every port Grayce would sail into. This sweet gesture by her new brother enabled her to make quite an impression with her new friends along the way. Grayce no longer sailed with anger. Enthusiasm and excitement was being generated everywhere that now fueled Grayce to fulfill her dreams. Her global and spiritual village was out there helping in the real world ways it could. More importantly, they were always holding loving thoughts for Grayce.*

*There is an Eye of powerful protection where the angels live that encircles this abstract world. Connect with the available energy in the Eye and you will be given wings to fly. In this blessed vortex where anything is possible, nothing impossible exists. Seek to be grace, give unconditional love and expect joy filled bliss in every moment. That is living on purpose and with intent.*

Grayce was quietly thrilled at the fun she was having distributing the **Think Love** bracelets. Wonder why I was so mad at Josh for so long over nothing? It is so much easier to just breath and let it all go. Maybe we should expand the idea? Or maybe I will just be OK trying to make things better and leave it at that. Will Josh tire of helping me? Confusion, it always exists in the overactive mind. Fine, I will just concentrate on sailing and Einstein. The puppy took to sailing like sugar in iced tea, a natural fit. Grayce rarely let him out of her lap. The two were inseparable now. Grayce said out loud, "I love you Einstein!" Ranger would definitely be proud. I bet he is wagging his doggie tail up in Heaven, she thought.

With that, Luca appeared. "Grayce, it is time we share any easy conversation about forgiveness. You have finally learned to forgive everyone fully, congratulations! It is your time now sweet one. The hardest one to forgive is ourselves. We are all perfectly imperfect. We all make human mistakes that are usually rather painful. Some more than others and that really doesn't even matter. Our mind punishes us with its fake sense of judgment. It's how the Creator designed it all so we could learn about the *REAL* truth of life. Life; it is really an epic adventure no where, that leads to now. All that matters for us all is right here, right now. When you find the precious path to self forgiveness, Grayce, painful learning will cease. Next, a bliss filled life begins. Grayce, this is all real. A sage has been born, indeed."

"Why do I have to spend so much time in forgiveness? I am tired of forgiving people. The bracelet idea is a success, Luca. That is amazing, wouldn't you agree? I am helping people and spreading the word of love. Besides, I don't have anything to forgive myself for, do I?" Luca just sat there as the warm, salty air left its trail on everything. In silence, Grayce stopped fighting the conversation. In the space of quiet, she began to cry. "I am sorry Luca. It's true I have been awful to myself. It is absolutely true you are right. Help me learn, Luca please?" Luca smiled.

*"Every hour you must learn to ask for forgiveness and you will receive it. You also forgive anyone who needs it, and then you slow time. As the day goes on, hour by hour, you keep forgiving. The gift is that the bondage of self incrimination evaporates in the face of forgiveness. You unshackle yourself from self imposed punishment and attach yourself to a kite string instead. You are meant to fly; we all are Grayce."*

*"Every hour you forgive, you just keep flying, higher and higher. Just like the perfect wind in sailing Grayce, you already know this. When sunset rolls around, you rest. Reflecting upon a day of forgiveness is the ultimate freedom. The absolute one great peace. It is simply everything. It connects you to your Creator and the Creator to you, forever. You will then simply fly on into eternity. Learn this fully Grayce and then learn no more. Just be. Just sail. Just fly."*

## Chapter Twenty-One

# JOURNEY HOME

Grayce neared the entrance for the Panama Canal. Holy Cow, she thought and laughed out loud. Wow, I really did this! She had consulted her Polynesian tarot cards earlier in the day. Grayce drew the Albatross card, undeniably establishing soaring confidence within. Einstein snuggled in her lap affirmed her total happiness. This was an official trip and it had been planned for over three years. Grayce was supposed to have unquestioned access granted for the *Silent Partner* to pass through. She was expected by the local officials and already knew which lock to proceed into. The canal itself was daunting, huge and impressive. She imagined how many people died trying to establish such a massive and innovative idea before such imaginative things were possible.

It was early morning, Grayce's favorite time of day. Still dark, a light marine layer mist gently filled the salty air. As she entered the first lock a smelly diesel boat pulled up with a very rude man yelling obscenities into a loud speaker. It was now raining and exactly 4:02 am. He was demanding Grayce get off her boat! This cannot be happening, she thought. All this way and now a paper work tussle? Unreal, but OK. I can do this. Breath and be calm. Stop talking. Listen. The man finally spoke in English informing Grayce she owed the $800. Panama Canal lock fee. Grayce could not pass through until the debt was settled. Exhausted, she grudgingly stepped off the *Silent Partner*.

Grayce then defiantly laid down on the dock and said; "I do not have $800. Arrest me."

Luca appeared at just the right time, once again. "Grayce I am here. Please remember, you are not alone. It is all right. Together we can do this." Grayce was in tears by now. "I do not have $800. Luca, is it possible that you do?" A long pause was interrupted by more shouting from Grayce. "Luca, what are you doing? I need money; not lecturing!" Luca undeterred by her ravings, slowly reached in his little shorts pocket and pulled out a dirty, old looking wad of bills wrapped in a red, rubber band. He handed the money to Grayce. She noticed it was not American currency and assumed it was Euro. She stopped crying.

"Here you go Grayce, the exact amount of currency you need for this epic passage. Exactly $800." More tears. "Luca I do not understand, how?" He giggled knowing his truth. "Miracles are our birthright, Grayce, seize them. This was the money I had saved from my newspaper route as a boy. My brothers were always borrowing newspaper money from me, like I was a bank. When I died it was in my pocket. How it remains now might be a mystery or it might be a miracle. You decide Grayce." There was nothing she could say except, "Thank you, Luca. Yes, please I accept your kind gift. I welcome this miracle. How absolutely sweet of you."

And, with that the *Silent Partner* was granted access to the intimidating Panama Canal. Seems all you need is a boat, some money and a really good angel onboard. It is really that easy. Grace must be given when asked. When grace is accepted, we easily create harmony. Einstein made his first debut riding solo up front. Grayce took a lot of photos to send back to her global village. She had collected quite a tribe on this trip. Staying connected had more meaning now, in a real, tangible way. She silently gave thanks for Mrs. Poe, Luca, Josh, Mrs. Heartworth, Lady Palm, and all the assorted angel's who had come to change her life. Luca joined Einstein up front. Grayce knew better than to try and capture Luca on film, he simply would not show up. He grinned and Grayce affirmed to never forget that smile. No camera needed. Luca had permanently imprinted her soul with infinite love and boundless joy.

"Grayce, did you know that the Panama Canal was formally opened in 1914? It is 48 miles long, connecting the Atlantic Ocean to the Pacific Ocean, with assistance from the Caribbean Sea. In 1914 there were approximately 1000 ships passing through the canal. Today over 15,000 pass through annually. Amazing, yes? Talk about creation. 1914 was exactly 401 years after Panama was first crossed by; Vaco Nunez de Baloboa'. Now, you are as much a part of history as anyone else. Young woman sailing solo around globe, yours is an impressive story, Grayce. Celebrate your accomplishment. You are brave, talented, and an expert sailor. Own your grace, you earned it girl! I love you, we all do."

Luca left without so much a good bye. Angels, come and then they simply go. They are here, they are everywhere. But you will never ever know where they are, unless you learn to trust them. Grayce had learned. She now knew, they had been here all along. Her anger had blocked them. Light is powerful, once it gets inside the dark cannot exist. Love filled her heart and soul. Nothing mattered now except being true to her own purpose, her calling. She was a sailor who cruised the ocean with **Awakened Grace.** As she left the Panama Canal, sailing back home to Key West, she was totally free for the very first time. Grayce laughed out loud and said; "Epic adventure to a life outside of the mind." She knew where she was going and understood it would have no permanent address. The world was now her playpen and the ocean was forever her playground.

It was several days' calm sailing before she caught her breath over the vastness that is the Panama Canal. It was daunting and majestic. Even if in a man made, concrete kind of way. There were also relentless thoughts about her own saga; the friends she had made along the way and the sudden loss of poor Ranger. She was finally becoming accustomed to finding her way through the tug-of-war of thoughts. They certainly seemed to have an endless supply of energy. The less time she fed the assaulting thoughts, the less importance they had over her mind. She contemplated grace. What does it actually mean? She thought about the word a while. Dolphins swam by and made contemplation a pleasure. Grace, it means honor, class, elegance, majesty, service, kindness. She held a transforming thought; ***my natural grace is awakening.*** She now understood intimately there is no grace in fear, doubt and worry. No, these self defeating thoughts actually were like pouring gasoline on a hot fire, it only speeds up the destruction of what is being burned.

Grayce liked the fact she was self correcting her thoughts now. Or was she? Perhaps it was a divine link being established? Was it Luca's magic? Was it the visit from her many assorted angels, Winston, Angus, Frances? What if she was just being self corrected by the universe? Oh, yes she liked that one. If I believe my life is always being self corrected by the Creator, then it stands to reason that I will never need to worry again! Is that even possible? She strangely had an immediate, strong desire to go swimming and had no idea why, it just was there.

Just then, not far off Key West, Grayce magically encountered an exceptionally large pod of humpback whales. There is nothing in the world quite like this feeling. Imagine twenty or more whales swimming along side a relatively small sailboat. It's absolutely amazing just how tiny you feel. Somehow, if you allow it, your spirit will actually become a part of the swimming pod. Whales swim fast too. This is definitely not a sailing endeavor for sissies. You can feel this fantastic energy. These massive souls, gently moving through the water like choreographed flexible, dancers in harmony. Grayce cracked herself up again, imagining these magical dancers masquerading as living submarines. A sailors dream, indeed.

Almost as fast as they were swimming, suddenly they stopped. The whole group just became entirely calm, weightless and totally still. Grayce began to cry. She knew this was a calling. It was time to swim in the water with these amazing creatures who had silently shared her incredible journey. This was something she had always dreamed of doing, however, fear prevented her from diving in. She recalled the Rumi quote Luca shared with her,

**The day that you were born, a ladder appeared to lead you home to Heaven.**

***My soul is from else where, and I intend to end up there." Rumi***

Grayce decided it was time to test her faith. She would dive in and swim with the gentle giants before her. It was a decision many would have encouraged her to avoid. There are many dangers in swimming with whales especially if they are migrating. Grayce took the dramatic chance anyway. She instructed Einstein to stay put, securing him to a tie down near the front of the boat where he loved to sleep. Grayce took time to consider something special her father, Angus had told her many years ago. Until recently, she had forgotten the conversation preferring to recall bad things instead. As she allowed the happy memories in, peaceful thoughts followed. Angus said,

*"Grayce, you are a Thoroughbred. You were born for racing the wind and swimming in the sea. You were born for riding beautiful horses in the sand and sun. Please, dear daughter, know you are a beautiful little girl. Cherish that part of you so that it might stay alive as you grow old. Lastly child, in all your innocence, never forget you, Grayce, are also regal and refined. Pegasus is your Guardian angel, Grayce. Pegasus is majestic and gray. A mighty winged horse who will always be divinely by your side."*

That explained the dream about Pegasus back on Great Abaco after the storm. Grayce giggled to herself, quietly giving thanks to Angus. She glanced over at Einstein, still sleeping. Grayce strapped on her mask and fins. Without hesitation, she dove into the water. The cool, salty water refreshed her senses and her mind within seconds. With clarity of mind, she opened her eyes to see the divine sight. It was there alright, the sun rays casting bright blue light on it all. The whales were a large family; this she already knew. The way they just floated in the water she did not know. It was pure love. Peace in the water. These supreme whales do not struggle, do not strain. No, instead what she saw is they simply allowed. Grayce wanted to be a part of this great peace so she just hovered there. It was simply perfect. Floating above them, as long as her human breath would allow, she gave the whales her deeply genuine thank you.

Returning to the surface for air, Grayce immediately made eye contact with Einstein. He was awake now, looking for her whereabouts. She inhaled the fresh air, took a deep breath and told the Creator thank you. She enjoyed the ocean water for as long as she wanted to and appreciated how free it made her feel. Recalling the *"Perceiving Freedom"* sculpture in Africa, a new respect for being free came over her. I guess we really are unshackled as soon as we choose. Realizing it was time to move on, Grayce reluctantly hauled herself out of the clear, blue, healing water. Tears flowed and she said thank you again. It was time to go home. She hoisted the main and jib sail on the *Silent Partner* once more. Grabbing up little Einstein, Grayce settled into the wind and appreciated it all.

Sailing was calm and easy. Time passed and Grayce was happy. Hungry and thirsty, she went down below for some water and food. Moments later, the angles returned. All of them. Returning to the deck from the galley kitchen, she could not believe her eyes. Grayce tried not to hyperventilate. Sitting right there, out of no where was Luca, Frances, Angus and Winston. "Hello dear Grayce, we are all so very proud of you! Look at the impressive global accomplishment you have singlehandedly achieved. Grayce was crying now as they all had a big, group hug. She sat down in between Angus and Frances. "This is so awesome you are all here! I just cannot believe it is my entire family all together again. I never dreamed this was possible."

Grayce was so happy she gushed; "I could not have done this without all of you. I used to think this was a solo journey. I now know I was dead wrong. My strength comes from knowing I am loved. With that, I can love others without fear of loss or being hurt. It has been so fun, super scary and even enlightening. Honestly, I do not think I ever want to live on the mainland. Sailing is my true passion. The ocean is my home." Angus smiled and said; "Dear Grayce, your home is wherever you decide it is. And now that you can accept grace in your life, you can go and do anything you want to. It doesn't have to be a struggle or a fight anymore. You do not have to be tougher than anyone else. Just know when to ask for help if you need it." She sighed, "You know Dad I remember you telling me that but I just forgot. Thank you for sending the Pegasus in my dream after the storm, I will always remember that." Angus gave her a big bear hug. "Grayce, you are welcome."

Frances added; "Dear daughter, you have so much grace and courage. It is going to take you far in your life. Tap into your feminine assets. Always remember to give back to others who assist you. Acknowledge your allies and treat them with love and kindness. It is always better to be kind than to be right. Let other people know more than you, even if you know more than them. And listen, I mean really listen. What you can hear and learn will change your life in all the best of ways. Those who just talk their way through everything miss what others can teach them. "Oh Mom, thank you. It is really fun to learn about grace from you, I am so happy you are here now." Frances bowed her head; I am always here with you Grayce, always."

Winston chimed in; "Dear granddaughter, we have always been so bonded. You are my favorite jewel in the world. It was fun to teaching you about the ocean and sailing. It is even more fun to see you take those talents out into the world and inspire other lives. The *Think Love* bracelet is really special. Grayce, I am so happy you care about others so much. I was so greedy in my life! To see you are *not* that way makes the Creator smile. Of course, the Creator smiles on you no matter what you do. It just means so much you have gone from flipping a sunfish sailboat in the Key West marina to sailing the globe and navigating the Panama Canal. Way to go girl! I love you." Grayce laughed a little recalling her young days sailing. "Thank you Grandfather, I love you too."

Luca was just grinning and said nothing. Grayce looked at him and said; "Little boy Luca, I will never know how you found me or why I deserved your love and protection. A little, Portofino born boy, in a dingy with $800. Euros in your pocket exactly when I needed it. You made all the difference for me Luca at every point in my sail. Thank you." Luca closed his eyes and said; "I love you Grayce. Angels see all human stories at once and we can intervene at will. Your story called to me because of your love for the ocean. I was compelled by your stubborn independence. I also loved your amazing dog Ranger. Angels simply get to pick who they want to help and when. It was our destiny to meet. Now we will never be apart. It is my honor, Grayce, I will always be by your side. Never forget that. Take good care of Einstein, he is special too." Grayce gave Luca a big hug and promised she would.

After the angels left, she cracked up when she realized it was 4:02 pm in the afternoon. What is it with this time thing? Now that grace had fully awakened in her, she no longer let the annoying thoughts about understanding time bother her. Acceptance and surrender had completely transformed her way of being in the world. Peace was her ally now, not fear or confusion. She trusted in the Creator's plan for her. She knew now it was OK if she did not know it all. Let it go, seek everything divine and follow the ways of nature. Old adage but absolutely spot on. She found her calm in the Eye. Grayce would never be the same again.

*Dolphins swam along the Silent Partner and an Albatross flew overhead. I know where I belong now. Mother Ocean thank you for being my home. My Creator above thank you for it all. Please show me the way home now. Grayce loved the fact it was still 4:02 pm and smiled. It just did not matter any more, the inconceivable and unexplainable time part of this epic journey. The wind was light and the salty air rejuvenated her senses once more. Time was irrelevant but sailing in faith was now everything. She knew it was all perfectly designed by the Creator and her guardian angels. Who could ask for more?*

After returning to Key West, there was quite a party for Grayce and Einstein at the marina. Mrs. Poe arranged everything, so there was an even a band from the local elementary school. All the kids knew Grayce and wanted to play for her. There were countless multi-colored balloons, Crab Cakes and Cole Slaw, Chocolate Cake, Pink Lemonade and Guava Punch. Reporters were there along with countless strangers and many well known friends. It was super cool to see that Josh and Mrs. Heartworth had traveled from Great Abaco to welcome Grayce back home. Lady Palm sent a huge bouquet of flowers. Looks like this new global village had certainly adopted Grayce and this new family gave her many reasons to smile. And, smile she did, again, and again and again. Jimmy Buffet was in town too and absolutely filled everyone with his beloved ocean themed, music of joy.

The great tune *"Nautical Wheelers"* by Mr. Buffet was the song of the day and Grayce smiled thinking how this simple song changed her life years ago. After giving the Christmas ornament to Jimmy and befriending him, Grayce her friendship with the celebrity no one else could ever have. Grayce loved to paint and so did Jimmy. After all the hoopla slowed down, the two united *Nautical Wheeler's*, swapped not only sea stories but a pencil drawing, and a water color, or two. Beyond cool, celebrities are really just like us, Grayce thought. She gave yet another heartfelt thanks for the magic of life. Gratitude works.

When Grayce slowly stepped off the boat, for the first time in over a year, she stood on the same dock she had walked down to begin her sail. She had little to say but was grinning, ear to ear. Grayce carried her new best friend, Einstein and he was a little overwhelmed by all the people. At the end of the pier she addressed the crowd. "I made it! Actually, we all made it! Don't you just love it when life creates more that your dreams could have ever imagined? The sailing was perfect. I can report I loved it all, even being temporarily blinded. While some of it was terrifying, the outcome is a renewed faith in my Creator, my angels, my new global tribe, and myself."

"You are so kind to be here to welcome my return, thank you all. Meet Einstein my new puppy! Isn't he just the best? After I almost gave up on love and hope, this puppy filled my heart back up with all I ever need. I found him in the Seychelles and will blog about the experience in more detail soon. Most of the trip has been recorded on my Facebook page so you know where I have been. What you don't know is I carried doubt about angels when I left. My experience has proven they not only exist; they protect us always. More than anything else, I now know their existence is unquestionably true."

My first encounter with an angel was most unexpected, I hit his dingy in the open sea. His name is Luca. And Luca loves the Persian poet Rumi. I will quote one of Luca's favorite Rumi quotes to summarize my feeling today. Even with Luca's physical absence, he knows every thought I have and hears every word. Thank you Luca. I love Rumi too now. Rumi the loving mystic writes;

> *"Don't grieve.*
> *Anything you lose comes around in another form.*
> *Knock and He'll open the door.*
> *Vanish, and He'll make you shine like the sun.*
> *Fall and He'll raise you to the Heavens.*
> *Become nothing, and He'll turn you into everything!"*
> *~Rumi~*

"My beloved angels taught me who I am, out on the ocean. My angels showed me that in any *EYE,* I always do matter. By the way, every one of you matter too." Grayce grinned and the audience applauded. "Never doubt the presence of an angel, as that sends them away. And, they do not like anger so remember to keep your temper in check. Today, I want to dedicate my epic sailing journey to my beloved Ranger and my faithful angels. I truthfully needed them all. I wrote a little something while sailing, so I will read it to you now."

*We go fast because we are afraid to fail.*

*Under our intense fears lie a sleeping joy.*

*Sleep brings peace.*

*Peace is just being.*

*Being gave birth to joy.*

*Love existed way before being.*

*When we succeed in ceasing to be superhuman or supremely blind, stubbornly self-willed, and allow love to change us, then we will find Heaven in the Eye of any storm.*

*The Eye teaches you acceptance and strength.*

*The Eye teaches you courage and joy.*

*The Eye teaches you to allow and stop fighting.*

*The Eye reminds you to laugh at yourself and quit judging everything.*

*The Eye is simply God awakening us and granting us his unwavering grace.*

*What you needed strength for before, is now absolutely being done for you.*

*Trust more, forgive, and allow it all.*

*This is truly ALL you will ever need to know about grace.*

*Now that grace has finally awakened my SPIRIT guides me now.*

*Experience a new way to live defined by you and the Creator.*

*Discover the reason for this journey called life.*

*The gift for your efforts, is called peace.*

*It exists in the Eye of your own creation.*

*It is the gift of pure love, a shared divine unity for us all.*

Awakening to her familiar sunrise over Key West, Grayce felt all grown up. It was a beautiful Sunday morning. She loved being home. There was a sweetness and a sadness, both were now alright. Einstein was watching the sun come up too. Grayce felt like taking a walk. "Let's go puppy, its time for some food." She grabbed up little Einstein, stepped off the *Silent Partner* and thought about town. Walking past the little coral where Angus's pony had been struck by lightning brought up many new memories from her heroic sail. She simply smiled. After exiting the marina gates, Grayce heard some intriguing music. She started walking down a dirt road she did not recall knowing before.

Grayce was a Key West born tomboy, a precious sight to behold. She walked barefoot, Einstein in her backpack, purple dreadlocks in her hair, cut off Levi shorts, and legs tan as a well worn saddle. A girl of summer, Grayce, was all year round. The music further compelled her and then she saw it; a small green church on the beach at the end of the road. As she strolled into the church of her dreams, the sun rays directed her gaze to a broken clock reading 4:02 am. Giggling, she contemplated the meaning of that and decided there was none. It did not have to make sense anymore.

The church was stunning. She felt right at home, it was pure peace. Grayce loved this place and wondered why it took so long for her to find it. Deciding to silence her thoughts and listen, her heart slowed and she closed her eyes. The choir of no description sang a Joni Mitchell song, *"Circle Game."* Grayce resolved to come back here next week and maybe introduce herself around. It amused her to know she sailed around the world only to come back home and still be surprised. Life is good and love is really all that matters.

> **Circle Game**
> *"And the seasons they go round and round*
> *And the painted ponies go up and down*
> *We're captive on the carousel of time*
> *We can't return we can only look*
> *Behind from where we came*
> *And go round and round and round*
> *In the circle game." Joni Mitchell*

# *Acknowledgements*

I would like to thank those people who have supported my writing endeavors. I hope you do not mind being in the back of the book. The dedication to Dr. Dyer had to be first, I know you will understand.

Thank you to my entire family for loving me and understanding my writing dreams.

Thank you to Christina Miles and Sharon Lee Dalkey. They both assisted me with editing and encouragement just when I needed it most.

Thank you to Julia Humason, whose unwavering faith in my writing kept me from giving up many times. Your friendship is irreplaceable.

Thank you to Judie Profeta and Christine Chin for proofreading and loving, moral support.

Thank you to Sue Wulfmeyer for being the best neighbor ever and for the prayers.

Thank you to Marsha Manion at Balboa press who ignited my fire to finally get this book published.

Thank you to Dr. Wayne Dyer, my favorite author ever! Your books inspire me to reach for excellence in all I do. Your guiding light is truly divine, bless you.

Printed in the United States
By Bookmasters